INTO THE DARKNESS

THE TWISTED LANDS SERIES

Book 1

STEVE CATTO

For all the lost souls

https://stevecattos.world

Artwork by More Visual

ISBN 978-0-9957298-1-0 e-book

ISBN 978-0-9957298-0-3 Paperback

Steve Catto Books

Prologue

The space between worlds consists of darkness.

It is widely thought, at least by intelligent beings, that darkness is an empty void, filled with nothing. This is, of course, a contradiction in terms.

The space between worlds is, in fact, filled with the whispers of countless collective consciousnesses, sometimes trying to make sense of the universe, but more often worrying about what their life-forms are going to do next.

Right at this moment, some of them are looking out across the endless void in search of a hero, and not all heroes ride over the crest of a hill on a horse wearing a suit of armour and waving a flag[1].

As luck would have it, they may have found one, but the first chapter of her story begins late one evening in a dirty city on a strange world, and plays out like a scene from an old black-and-white nineteen-sixties' gangster movie.

Watch carefully... there will be questions afterwards.

---

[1] The hero, not the horse

1 - If We Could

The lump of concrete smashed through the window, shattering it into thousands of fragments, which cascaded across the footpath and lay there, sparkling in the light from the street lamps.

A beacon flashed on the wall above the shop and an alarm began to bleat.

Two large figures crunched their way over the carpet of glass chunks, grabbing handfuls of jewellery, watches and rings, and stuffing them into bags.

The one with the curly hair looked across at the one with the greasy face and grunted.

"Right then. The boss'll be pleased with this lot. Wot's next?"

His mate glanced behind them. A black van had just rounded the corner and was stopping across the road from where they were standing.

"There he is!" he exclaimed.

The boss stayed in the driver's seat, and another hefty looking man jumped out of the passenger door and ran across to help collect up the bags.

"The cops'll be a while yet," he said to them both, as he threw the last bag into the back of the van and closed the doors. "You go and hit the other place around the corner now, like we planned."

He jumped back into the passenger seat and the van sped away, leaving Curly-top and Greasy-face to make their own way to the next target on foot.

The team liked to work that way. The boss had always found it was better to have runners on the ground keeping an eye out for trouble, rather than having everybody shut in the back of the van where they could all get caught together. That also meant he got to keep out of the way, and just turn up in the van to load it when each job was done.

It wasn't particularly cold that night, the streets were deserted, and walking was better than being cooped up in the back of a smelly van.

Anyway, they liked being paid to look for trouble.

As the two henchmen rounded the corner, they saw the figure of a boy appear from behind one of the dustbins on the opposite side of the road ahead of them. An arm reached out and pulled him back out of sight.

"That's those kids again!" grunted Curly-top, hoarsely. They'd seen the children before, on other nights. They were a nuisance.

"Yeah. I think it is," agreed Greasy-face, squinting down the road. It was well lit. If it was the pesky children, they had them trapped. There wasn't anywhere else along the road where they could hide, and it was a dead end because it went downhill to the railings by the river. The city was riddled with alleyways and most of them were dead ends.

The other job would have to wait. The boss would be really pleased if they caught these two.

"Let's get 'em," he growled.

As they both started towards the dustbins, two small shadows broke away and ran down the road towards the river. Curly-top turned back to cover the left-hand side of the street, while Greasy continued across the road to follow them.

They looked in all the doorways along the way. The doors had writing on them that said things like 'Smithson and Monk – Solicitors at Law' and 'R. J. Pennyworth – Photography'. None of those places were worth robbing, they just contained paperwork and petty cash. Money shops and jewellers were best.

Some doorways were deeper, and their doors were set back further from the road, but none of them were especially dark, and it was easy to see that no-one was hiding in them. Curly-top passed by the window of the other shop that was their intended target for the next job. For a moment he considered whether it might be better just to do the job and forget about the children, but he hadn't brought anything to smash the window with, and his mate was already further down the road anyway.

Just then the van pulled up across the top of the junction. The boss had driven around the block and was expecting them to have finished the next job.

The driver shouted something, and they both turned to answer him.

The children, who had been hiding between two parked cars, took that distraction as an opportunity to run back up the middle of the road, away from the men and towards the van. It was the only way of escape.

Curly-top and Greasy-face were skilled in many things, mostly involving theft, robbery, threats, extortion and menacing people. Running uphill wasn't on the list.

The passenger had seen the chase and was getting out of the van as the children approached it. They split up. It was a good tactic, widely used by prey to avoid capture when there was only one hunter. The girl ducked around the front of the van, and the boy tried to run around the back. The passenger threw himself at the boy, pulling him to the ground, before dragging him upright and twisting his arm behind his back.

By this time the two henchmen had caught up enough to see what was happening.

"That's the boy we saw by the bins," panted Greasy-face, leaning on his knees in an attempt to recover from his unexpected bout of exercise. "Where's the other kid?"

They dragged the boy round to the other side of the van and stood talking to the boss, who had remained in the driver's seat.

"She went round the front. I think she must have gone over there somewhere," he said, waving his hand vaguely across the intersection towards more shops and doorways.

"What shall we do with them, Boss?" asked the passenger, who still had the boy in an arm-lock.

"You can kill the boy!" he said ferociously. "But fetch me that girl! I know people who'll buy girls. She's worth money!"

Curly-top strode away purposefully across the road and Greasy-face lumbered along after him, still trying to catch his breath. The passenger opened the back of the van and climbed in, dragging the boy with him, and slammed the doors.

From the driver's seat of the van, The Boss watched his henchmen as they tracked carefully up the road, searching in the doorways. This area was well-lit too, just like the other road. It didn't look as if there was anywhere to hide here either.

The alarm that was still bleating outside the shop where they had done the first raid was beginning to annoy him, and it was bothering him too for some strange reason. It wasn't particularly loud, but it was affecting his brain. It didn't even sound right anymore. It was honking, but the silences in between were somehow noisy too. Like when you've been up the club all night listening to loud music, he thought. The silence isn't silent, it hisses. He batted himself on the ear and looked perplexed. It hadn't made any difference, except his ear now hurt. Thudding noises were coming from the back of the van now, and he could hear muffled screams. His colleague was obviously enjoying whatever he was doing to the boy, but he was being too noisy. What had started out as a routine evening of smash and grab was going wrong, and his brain hurt. He turned around and thumped on the bulkhead with his fist. The noises from the back of the van stopped, but the alarm didn't. There was still a mysterious hissing in his ears.

And now he peered along the road. Curly-top and Greasy-face were wandering about aimlessly. They appeared to be making no progress in finding the girl.

In his side mirror the Boss saw a car approach and turn along the road behind him, towards the smashed-up shop. That wasn't the cops, he thought, it was probably the owner of the business, but the cops wouldn't be far behind. It was a shame they couldn't have done the other job and set off another alarm. That was always a good plan. Confusion, and more than one incident to deal with. Spread people out thinly, that was the trick. But now it was his men that were all split up, and the alarm would be attracting attention. They needed to be leaving. He shouted across to them to give up looking for the girl, and they turned towards him.

"There she is!" yelled Greasy-face.

The girl was kneeling on the ground near the back of the van. When he shouted, she sprang up, sprinted across the road to the footpath, and began to run along the front of the shops and offices. It was a comic sight. They were lumbering towards her, and she was running towards them, just like a scene from an old slapstick movie.

That was stupid, thought Curly-top, there wasn't anywhere she could go.

As she ran, she was glancing in each doorway. No, that was too wide. That was too bright. These weren't deep enough. But the girl had a plan, and Curly-top and Greasy-face didn't. While she'd been crouched by the van, she thought she'd seen an opening a bit further up the road that seemed ideal for what she wanted to do. It was just a question of getting to it before they got to her.

Suddenly, the noise of the alarm ceased. The owner of the shop must have reset it she thought as she ran. That was good because it was now quieter, and that always helped. Now all she needed was some darkness.

The two henchmen had started to slow down. The girl was still running as fast as she could, straight towards them, so there seemed to be no reason to hurry. She was just going to run straight into their arms.

As she got nearer to them, she recognised the place that she'd seen - on her right - the little opening that looked like it used to be an alleyway but was now blocked off part way along. There was a pair of stone pillars each side of a gap in the buildings. She swung herself around the corner into it. Yes, it was ideal! Solid walls, and no street lights directly in front of it. It went back six or seven steps to an old wooden door, which was painted green. In the dim light it was possible to see that the old paint was flaking, especially around the panels where the frame moved with the changing weather. Painted on it, in faded white lettering, were the words:

Backpacker's Hostel

She turned around, just in time to see the two men appear at the opening of the alleyway in front of her. From inside the van, further back along the road, came more muffled sounds of crying and screaming.

The greasy one leered at her.

"We've got you now," he growled.

She looked up at their faces in what light was managing to trickle past them from the street. They were used to dealing with people who were terrified of them, but she didn't seem to care, which they thought was strange. Dealing with someone who looked helpless but was, in fact, fearless, wasn't something they encountered from day-to-day, so they didn't understand it. The crying and screaming that had been drifting across the road from the van stopped.

"Sounds like that's the end of your little friend," said Curly-top, with a big yellow grin.

"Yeah, but you're coming with us. We know people who'll pay a lot of money to do interesting things to little girls, before they kill them very slowly," said the greasy one, creeping further towards her. "Even grubby little girls," he added, with a sneer.

They had now almost completely blocked out what little light was originally leaking into the old alleyway from the street. The alarm had stopped, the screaming had stopped, and the world around her was dark and silent.

Curly-top stuck his head over the other one's shoulder to take a better look at her in the shadows.

"Oooh, and you're a pretty one!" he said.

She looked at them both defiantly with her big dark eyes. The problem was that the two men thought everyone was scared of them. She ought to be terrified by now, but she didn't seem to be. They didn't know what to make of that. She was trying to look past them, as if hoping to find some way to escape, but there wasn't one.

After a moment she seemed to come to a conclusion. Her attitude changed. She slumped a little and held her hands out in what looked like a half-hearted shrug. "Yeah, we've got you now," thought the greasy one. The little girl looked up at them again before taking a big breath, followed by an equally big sigh.

"I'm sorry," she said, apologetically.

They were used to their victims apologising to them once they had realised the game was up. People usually had a change of heart and thought they could bargain. Most pleas for mercy began with the words "I'm sorry". It never worked. To an onlooker though, it could just as easily have sounded like the kind of apology someone would make when they had been left with no choice, and were being forced into doing something terrible which they would subsequently regret, but probably not very much, and not for very long.

Very slowly she took two steps backwards, deeper into the darkness.

"Aww..." said Greasy-face, baring a set of yellow decaying teeth in a supercilious grin. "She's *sorry*... how sad!"

At that, he leapt forwards into the void to grab the troublesome little pest, but his questing hands met with only stone walls and a wooden door. No-one was there! He stepped backwards in panic and reached behind him to push his mate aside.

"Get out of the way!" he moaned, "I can't see anything – she's not here!"

"I *am* out of the way!" called the curly one, from just outside the opening. "HOLY SHIT!"

Now startled, the greasy one turned. There didn't seem to be much light from the street lamps outside any more. He took a couple of steps to join his mate who was standing on the footpath near one of the stone pillars, gazing in disbelief at the surroundings.

There wasn't much light from the street lamps anymore because there weren't any street lamps. Here and there, wrought iron baskets on poles held burning logs, their smoke drifting gently upwards into a dark grey sky, and the flickers of flame making yellow and orange patterns dance on the wet cobblestoned ground.

They looked across towards the buildings on the other side of the road, and the junction with the little street that went downhill to the river, where the van should have been, but there were no buildings, and there was no junction and there was no van. The ground ahead of them was much wider than before and was littered with crates and sacks and barrows.

Masts and rigging reached upwards into the sky and the air was filled with smoke and smells. Dozens of people were milling around, shouting and moving boxes and bags, on their backs and on carts. Strangely dressed folk were standing around in small groups, talking. Merchants, sailors, drunkards and the odd person in uniform all moved about their various businesses.

Greasy heard a noise behind him and spun around. To his surprise, the alleyway behind them wasn't completely dark anymore and there was no door. Instead, a path curved away into the distance, lit by lamps hung from iron brackets on the walls. Openings led off to places unknown. Here and there someone carried a sack or pushed a cart.

He turned back to face the dockyard. Neither of them spoke, because there was nothing to say.

A merchant pushed past them into the street from behind, accidentally clouting Grease's ankle with the wheel of his barrow. The merchant grunted something that sounded like an apology. Greasy pulled him away from his barrow by whatever he could find that resembled lapels and held him up against the wall, banging his head.

"Wossallthisthen," he shouted at the poor frightened man. "Wossappened? Owdweget'ere?"

The little merchant's eyes glazed over in terror. He had no answers, even if he'd understood the questions. Curly-top took his mate by the arm in an attempt to calm him down and the merchant wriggled free, before scurrying away across the dockyard with the metal-rimmed wheels of his barrow rattling on the cobbles.

There was still nothing either of them could say. They watched dumbfounded as a man tied three sacks together by their necks and swung them off the deck of a ship on a wooden arm. Across to their left, two merchants were haggling over the price of six small, squawking crates. They were pointing and gesticulating. It wasn't clear what language was being spoken, but they didn't understand it.

When their gaze moved across again to the far side of the docks, they noticed the little merchant that Greasy had assaulted. He was standing near the gangplank of a particularly foreboding black ship, talking to three fearsome looking men dressed in dark clothes and boots, and sporting long beards. They appeared to be in possession of enormous swords.

The two henchmen looked up more closely at the ship. A small black and white flag was flying lazily in the rigging.

The big men were bending over the merchant, who was holding one of them gently by the lapels and making faces at him. Then he rubbed the back of his head. One of the men spoke to him again briefly and the merchant pointed accusingly across the dockyard, towards the entrance to the alleyway where Curly-top and Greasy-face were standing. One of them slapped the merchant heartily on the shoulder and grinned at him. Then they turned, and began striding across the cobblestoned yard towards the alleyway with great purpose.

Curly-top and Greasy-face looked around at their exciting new world with awe, and probably for the last time.

They were employed to look for trouble.

Today had been a success.

They had found it.

After a few moments the girl stepped out of the doorway into the shadows of the street.

The Boss was still looking around anxiously for his two henchmen. He couldn't see them anywhere and, from the distance, came the unmistakable sound of police sirens. He called out of the window but there was no reply, so he started the engine. There was still no trace of the two men. He called again.

It was just possible now to see the faint flashing of blue lights on the walls of the nearby buildings. He began to drive away, but the van wouldn't go properly. It moved, but he couldn't steer it. It hit the kerb and got stuck, but he managed to reverse it. Then he revved up the engine and tried to speed away, but the van swerved across the road and crashed into a dustbin.

Now a police car rounded the corner and screeched to a halt behind the crippled van. Two officers got out and went to speak to the driver. Then another police car appeared, and came to a halt across the road near the junction. The officers from that unit went to speak briefly with the others and then started to walk around the van. As one of them reached out to open the back doors, his foot crunched on a small plastic object which had been left on the road. He kicked it aside absent-mindedly. It rolled a little way and went down a nearby drain. Then his fingers turned the handle of the doors, pulled them open, and suddenly the calm of the evening erupted into scuffles and shouting.

In the ensuing commotion the girl slipped away unnoticed and started to make her way along one of the roads that led down towards the river.

As she walked, she reached into her pocket and produced two more of the little plastic objects. She didn't know why she'd kept them really, it was just best to tidy things away if possible, so that nobody asked any awkward questions. She'd lost one, it had rolled away where she hadn't been able to reach it, but it didn't matter. Nobody would think anything of it, even if they noticed it.

Further along the road, she dropped them carefully into a bin.

She couldn't think of any use she might have, either now or in the foreseeable future, for the dust caps from two tyre valves.

After a few minutes of walking, the flashing lights and sounds of commotion behind her had faded away in the distance, and the world had become dark and quiet again. She had spent most of her life in the darkness and the silence, it felt comfortable to her. This world didn't, and she'd often thought that the only reason people stayed in places like this was because they couldn't get away from them.

She turned down another small alleyway in the middle of a city block, which served as the access to the back of some tenements and restaurants, and picked her way between the bins and old mattresses which had been unceremoniously dumped there by the denizens of this dirty concrete city.

At the entrance to a hole at the bottom of a wall, behind a bin, a large rat nibbled industriously on a discarded brown apple core and watched her with interest. The rat didn't know what people actually did when they went down its alleyway, but they always came back out again, sometimes breathless and giggling, but occasionally on a stretcher, or sometimes in a bag. Hardly anyone went down there on their own, unless they were lost. This should be interesting to watch.

Another job done, she thought, as she made her way along the dirty ground towards the wall at the end of the alleyway, avoiding the potholes and gratings. All endeavours came at a price, everyone knew that. Sometimes the price was higher than others, but you had to pay it if you wanted the job done.

This time, the price had been her companion.

There was nothing more for her to do here. She would have to go home now and hope that everything was still alright there. This task had taken her longer than she had expected. It was supposed to have been a nice little trip to see how this world was progressing, but then she'd got involved with the boy, which had been nice – she didn't manage to get involved with boys very often these days – but then she'd stumbled across some very nasty goings-on which weren't the way she thought civilised people ought to behave. Perhaps she had succeeded in fixing some of them. Perhaps not, but she had been away too long. It would be a relief to leave this all behind now and spend some time in relative comfort.

The rat watched her shadowy form disappear slowly into the darkness, and waited for it to return, but it didn't.

After what seemed like an eternity it gave up, and scurried along the bottom edge of the wall to investigate.

When it got to the end of the alleyway it looked around suspiciously at the stonework, and then up towards the sky, before finally twitching its whiskers.

People know that rats are intelligent, and can see very well in the dark, even by the light of a few stars, but nobody knows whether they understand the meaning of the word 'puzzled'.

2 - Home At Last

It was somewhat disconcerting when you moved between worlds.

To go to a specific time and place you needed to concentrate your thoughts, and convince yourself you really were where you wanted to be, which of course meant you had to know exactly where you were going,

Getting home was always easy. She had favourite places that she could bring to mind very clearly.

The girl reached out to her left in the dark, until her hand touched the cold wall. It wasn't the damp, gritty wall of the alleyway.

At some time in the history of this particular world, human beings had started to construct a drainage scheme consisting of a maze of huge underground pipes and tunnels that went deep into a hillside. They were intended to empty water out into big concrete chutes that ran down the side of the valley, like ski ramps.

For one reason or another they had never completed it, so the passages going deep into the hillside just finished at walls of earth and stones, which was good because it made the whole system dry and safe.

This was home.

Somewhere around waist height her fingers found a shelf with a lighter and candle on it. The pattern of notches carved along the front edge of the shelf confirmed that she was near the end of T3, just where she had imagined she would be.

She struck up a flame and lit the candle. It was a relief to get away from that horrible smelly world. She went away to strange places too often. Something would have to be done about that, she thought.

The idea of a nice warm bed was always very tempting after being away, but there were other more pressing things that needed to be done first.

She had responsibilities.

When she had first found this place, the inside of the pipes and tunnels had been grey featureless concrete. It was the perfect place to use as a canvas for her work. In the yellow light of the candle the curved walls of the tunnel glowed and flickered with thousands of symbols and drawings. They stretched away from her into the gloom in both directions.

She had been working on them for years, and looking after them properly was a full-time job. Having to go away and leave them had been a nuisance. For the moment, sleep would have to wait.

She had worlds that needed tending to.

The light from the candle threw a halo around her silhouette as she worked her way along the tunnel, pausing every now and again to examine a particular area of the wall or ceiling.

She always seemed to be able to conjure up some piece of charcoal or mudbrick to sketch with, which was why she was perpetually grubby. Sometimes she would embellish something, or rub a bit of it out, or just caress it thoughtfully.

On closer inspection the marks were not just a continuous mass of symbols, they were arranged in clumps or groups, with a space around each collection.

In one particular spot she stopped to look at a few smudgy symbols that had been scratched with charcoal. She remembered drawing them a long time ago, and her mark was in the middle of them. The background appeared to have developed a faint tinge of colour. After a moment's thought, she added two new symbols to the collection, reinforced a few lines on the other symbols that had become faded, and very carefully blended their edges into the background so they became inseparable from the rest of the drawing. That seemed to satisfy her, and she set off again.

After a few minutes, she stopped at a section of wall that contained a particularly large and complex group of symbols.

The clump she was looking for was here... somewhere. She searched for a while longer before she found it. Yes, here it was! She put the candle down on the ground to allow her to examine the drawing in more detail.

On and off she'd been watching this one for quite a long time. It had always looked promising because it had the stylised symbols for earth, wind, water and fire, so there would be mountains, and rocks, and rivers and seas and clouds. But it wasn't black and white and grey like most of the others, it had colours. That meant it was a world that contained life. More importantly, it had symbols for lots of different kinds of grass and trees and animals. It had blues and greens and yellows and ochres. That meant it didn't just have simple life, it had complex life.

Worlds that had complex life in them were interesting, but troublesome.

On the one hand it was nice to see them grow, but on the other hand it meant someone had to look after them, and the biggest problem with things growing was that they kept needing more and more room.

This one had grown quite a bit while she had been away trying to sort out those stupid men in the city. The colours had developed into a pattern that was particularly appealing. She liked it.

There was still room for it to grow more, and if it did start to get too big, the nearest one to it was just a few scratchings of rocks and water. She could rub that one out to make space, it wasn't very important.

She looked at it thoughtfully with her head on one side. Did it need anything else? No, she didn't think so. Not right now. She'd put enough different kinds of trees and animals in it, there wasn't any need to add more, in fact, some of them could go really, and that might slow down its rate of growth a bit. The funny tree thing with the long trunk and the sticking out branches at the top had been an experiment. The symbol for that was getting bright, so there were a lot of them. There was also the animal with the really long tail. That was just annoying, and a bit silly really. They didn't seem connected to anything else, so they probably didn't do much, and this world needed the space.

She licked her finger and rubbed out the symbols for the funny tree and the animal with the long tail. It took a moment or two for her to get rid of the outlines of them, and they still left a mark where they had been, but the spaces were now little pools of smudgy grey in an ocean of colours.

Erasing the symbols for the tree and the animal wouldn't mean that all those types of tree and animal just disappeared, of course. She wasn't killing anything, it just meant that the world couldn't make any more of them.

She blended the edges of the colours carefully into the new empty patches with her fingertips, before standing back and looking at it again. That was better! The colours would grow into the gaps, and that meant the edge of the world wouldn't expand quite so quickly, so the little scratchy one next to it was safe for a while longer. It probably deserved a chance, she thought.

With that, she collected up the candle and resumed her journey. The worlds appeared to sense her presence as she approached them, standing out more proudly on the face of the walls, and glowing a little brighter in the light of the flame, as if reaching out to her in the hope of receiving some attention, and then sinking back again with an air of disappointment as she passed them by.

After a long time, she came to what appeared to be the end of the tunnel, but it wasn't a wall of earth and stones. It was a junction. To the left and right, a wider passageway curved off into the distance. Its walls were also covered in symbols and drawings, and every few steps along it was a junction that led to another tunnel.

There weren't just thousands of drawings stretching off into the distance.

There were millions of them.

***

A few hours later she was standing at the end of one of the pipes that projected out over the valley, looking particularly bedraggled and holding the stub of a dying candle. She made a mental note to take some more out with her next time and replenish the supplies on the shelves that were dotted around throughout the complex. Putting those up on concrete walls had taken her some time. She'd once seen someone using a little machine to put things up on concrete walls in one of the worlds she'd visited, and had stood and watched them for a long time until they'd eventually gone away to have some lunch. Someone, somewhere, was probably still wondering where their hammer drill had gone. It was noisy and it made a lot of dust, but it was better than nothing.

A sky full of stars twinkled through the gaps in the creepers that grew over the open end of the pipe. She had put a wooden floor down in this area which made the ground flat to walk on instead of curved. There was a bed here, a little table with two chairs, and a wood burning stove with a kettle on it.

In total she had managed to look at about a quarter of her worlds. Towards the end she'd been moving like the walking dead, and not giving everything the care and attention it deserved. She had probably missed some important things, and some of the decisions she had made along the way were possibly hasty and poorly considered. That wasn't fair, it wasn't a respectful way to treat your creations. She was tired. It was time for bed, and tomorrow would bring another day.

The ancients that once inhabited this area had made a living by fishing and trading, and they had built boats by hollowing out trees. It was a good way to make a container. Her bed was exactly that, a piece of hollowed out tree trunk.

She had made it herself many years ago, after she'd discovered this complex of pipes and tunnels. It had a curved bottom on the inside to give it the nice, rounded feeling of a hammock. A few layers of blanket to sleep on made it soft, and the contours hugged around her when she covered herself up, so the effect was like being in a cocoon. It felt exactly the way she had left it three months ago.

It was reasonable to assume that some of the life in her drawings looked at their skies now and again and wondered how their world worked. Perhaps only intelligent beings even suspected that she existed. If they did, they probably expected more from her, but there was only so much you could do. You couldn't live their lives for them.

Even an Ayla had to have a good night's sleep from time to time.

With that final thought, she put the candle on a small shelf near her head, blew out the flame, pulled the covers around herself and snuggled deeper into the little warm pit.

Behind her, in the empty maze of concrete tunnels, hundreds of inquisitive minds stirred and whispered to each other by the slowly flickering light of a thousand glowing worlds.

3 - The Long Shadow

Moonlight shining through a tiny window encrusted with dirt, and covered in cobwebs, percolated down into an otherwise darkened room, casting a pale dim glow on an old desk, at which a small figure could be seen sitting, its fingers tapping impatiently on the wooden surface.

It wasn't uncommon for the leader of The Council to request a one-to-one with her deputy before a full meeting. It usually gave them both a chance to discuss any outstanding issues, and decide on a strategy. Number Six didn't mind, it was part of the job, but her boss was never on time. In some societies, arriving a few minutes after something was due to start was perceived as being 'fashionably late'. Number Six however had always suspected it was just an excuse to make a pretentious entrance, so everyone knew you had arrived.

As if to support her suspicions, an ominous creak was heard from the shadows at the far end of the room, and a few seconds later the tall, gaunt figure of Number One appeared, dressed in a shiny black robe with matching hood and carrying an oil lamp. She strode purposefully to the desk and hung the lamp reverently on an iron stand which had been positioned in such a way as to cause the glow from the lamp to encircle the scene in an island of yellow light. She then produced a folder from the recesses of her robe, which she put down carefully on the desktop, before taking her seat opposite Number Six.

Of course, the robes and the lamp served little or no practical purpose, but she had always considered appearances and perceptions to be as important as actions and words.

"So, we are still no nearer to discovering what this *thing* is, or how it came to exist," she said across the desk to her deputy, in a chirpy, brittle voice that did not disguise the intensity of the frustration she felt at the lack of progress with the current situation, nor the disdain that she harboured for anyone who was involved with it, and most people who weren't.

Number Six shook her head sadly in the gloom. This was not the best environment for looking at reports, and she had often wondered why Number One insisted on conducting meetings in this way when the room was fitted with a perfectly good electric light, which could be operated using a switch by either door.

"Progress is being made," she said calmly. "More worlds have since been affected by it, but investigating these things is difficult. Eliminating such a creature is bound to require skills, and time," she added. "Skills that I fear we do not have."

"And time, which we also may not have," said Number One, pointedly. "There is still no news from the last group of agents that I sent to destroy it."

"Well, I told you that they were the wrong people for the job, and you didn't take any notice of me!" complained Number Six, bravely.

Number One shot her a stare, which was hardly visible in the gloom, and therefore had no effect.

"Perhaps," she said sharply, "but it seems you are having no luck finding anyone better. We are making no progress contacting this Ayla whom you insist is capable of solving the problem. Nobody seems to be able to find her," continued Number One, "and you say that you know her well."

Number Six shrugged, and raised her eyebrows.

"She has cut herself off from most of the world these last few years. It is not so much a question of contacting her, but more a case of approaching her in a way which will persuade her to help us."

This was an uncomfortable concept for Number One, who was used to people doing as they were told. As far as she was concerned, everybody soon found great enthusiasm for helping her when presented with options, one of which involved some rope, a whip and a barrel full of water. Given the latest news, or lack of it, her choice of actions was somewhat limited, but advice was something she was not accustomed to taking.

"You know I am not convinced that sending a fellow Ayla to investigate the problem is a workable idea. Nevertheless," she said carefully, "assuming she can be found, are you certain there is a way you can persuade her to cooperate?"

Number Six appeared to consider this for an unusually long time.

"I think so," she replied eventually. "But it'll take some organising. I need to explore various options, and I might be away for some time."

Number One spread her hands out on the desk and leaned across menacingly towards her deputy until their noses nearly touched.

"Well, do it then! Or find someone who can! I am sure we will manage without you," she said, bitterly.

"I'm sure you will," countered Number Six defiantly, rising from the chair and making her way casually towards the door behind her. "Despite your misgivings, contact the names on the list I gave you last week. Invite them to a meeting if you like, and they'll vouch for my choice."

Number One gritted her teeth, and directed a well-practised laser death-stare at the back of the departing figure's head as she crossed the floor, opened the door carefully and left the room, closing it gently behind her with the tiniest of clicks.

They were all useless, she thought, but her deputy was the most intelligent and forward-thinking of the entire council, and with that intelligence came dangers. Number One had always detected signs of rebellion, and a desire to take over the leadership. More recently she had become increasingly dependent on Number Six to get even the most basic things done, and tonight she had found herself taking orders from her.

This could not be allowed to continue, but once Number Six had succeeded in recruiting this Ayla, she would be surplus to requirements and could be disposed of somehow. Perhaps she could be made to disappear without trace, which was the usual fate reserved for traitors, otherwise the trick would be to make her death look like an accident.

Number Six might believe she would be away for some time.

If she had anything to do with it, Number Six would not be coming back at all. She was not used to dealing out retribution personally, but despite the unfortunate events of recent weeks she still had ways to arrange it.

The first step however was to ensure that the Ayla recommended by Number Six was recruited and deployed, and up to the task.

After shuffling through her papers, and making some notes, she rose from the chair, returned the folder to its pocket deep in her robe, and walked slowly away from the desk, holding the lamp out at arm's length in front of her, so that her outline cast a long dark shadow on the ground in the flickering light as she disappeared into the depths of the room.

Appearances and perceptions were important. Even when nobody was watching.

4 - Morning

Morning found the little girl sitting at the table in her room overlooking the valley, holding a mug of tea, and feeling somewhat refreshed.

She had pulled back the vines and creepers that served as a curtain, and was taking in the sunshine, and the view of the treetops and the old brown river that snaked away into the distance. Being back home was always pleasant, even though there was work to be done. It would take a couple more good sleeps before she was fully recovered from her trip away though.

That was the worst part of being an Ayla. The art and the drawing and the subsequent tweaking were great. Watching your worlds growing and evolving was very rewarding, but the travelling was crap.

She took a big drink from her mug.

You could tell a lot of things about your worlds just by looking at their drawings, but you didn't know exactly what was happening inside them without actually going there. Sometimes, you found things you didn't like, and then it was hard to leave without doing something about them. Even though it wasn't really your personal responsibility to meddle with the inner workings of your creations, it was still a difficult choice, whether to ignore things that you found, or try to fix them.

Perhaps a conscience wasn't something that you could afford if you wanted to be a creator of worlds.

Creating them was the easy part. In the beginning you drew symbols for things like earth, wind and fire to make a prototype world, and it got earth, wind and fire. It was a simple as that. Oh, and rocks of course. They were useful. Any decent world ought to have rocks. And water, that was good too. You soon got the hang of what you needed after you'd done it a few times.

Then you left them. You planted the seeds and you left them, and at some time, if you were lucky, they would grow. They started to develop colour, which was a sign of life. At first it would usually be blue, and only faint, perhaps hardly noticeable against the background. It wasn't much of a world at that stage, you had to leave it longer. After a while it might grow stronger and other colours would appear, usually greens and purples. They were different kinds of life, but they still didn't have any real form, they were just like dust. All they did was to multiply and make more dust.

That was when the real art began. Anybody could plant the seeds of a world, but sculpting it into something pleasing was a different thing altogether, and very much a matter of personal taste.

Learning the primary symbols wasn't difficult, there weren't many of them and they were pretty obvious. They looked like what they were. Triangles were rocks, wavy lines were water, a spiral was wind.

Once you had managed to strike up life you needed to organise it, and that was where the secondary symbols came in.

They didn't actually create anything, they just provided a form around which other life could grow, and that was why some of the other Aylas called them templates. When she organised life she usually started off with grass and trees. Other forms of life seemed to need them, they grew much better if they had grass and trees. If you wanted a specific type of tree you could draw it very accurately, but if you just wanted trees of a general shape you could draw a fuzzy template and you'd get things that might be quite different in their details, but still all looked basically like trees.

The same was true of animal life. If you wanted creatures with four legs and a tail, you could draw something which looked vaguely like that, and life would form itself into a variety of creatures that had four legs and a tail.

Sometimes you might get bored and fancy trying a very specific and accurately modelled life form, something that might be viewed as being unique. Most of the time you finished up rubbing it out because it didn't work well. Life didn't like specifics, it liked generalisations, so you ended up drawing accurate representations of the symbols for your basic materials like water, earth and rocks, but you drew fuzzy templates to organise your life.

When you started a world, you always began by drawing your mark, so that everyone knew whose world it was. Of course, all the ones she drew started with 'JM' in the middle.

That was useful because, every now and again, you would be asked to look after someone else's worlds, or another Ayla would come to look after yours. Convention dictated that you were supposed to change and maintain other people's worlds in keeping with their visions and style, but there was an unwritten understanding that you were allowed to draw a world of your own somewhere amongst theirs, as payment for your work, and they would subsequently tend to it for you.

Some Aylas were always off gallivanting and were rarely at home, so their collections of work were often left in the care of a friend, and had become a mishmash of really odd styles. She had always been very diligent. She rarely went away for more than a few weeks, and nothing needed urgent attention in that space of time, so it had hardly ever been necessary to delegate the upkeep of her work to anyone else.

The previous trip had been too long. Had she known she was going to be away for months she may well have chosen to get someone in, but that was the last resort. There was still the drawing of a world somewhere in the depths of the pipe marked T72 that had the initials 'BG' in the middle of it. It was covered in moons and stars and glitter, and decorated with sparkles. It looked like a fairy had been sick on the wall. That was the first, and last, time that she would invite Ayla

Goodison to house sit. Good old Belinda. She'd left crystals in the room as well.

In truth there weren't many people that she'd be happy to leave in charge of the place. She had always kept herself to herself and didn't have many friends. There was Ayla Mubara, Mabel, she was okay, but tended to over-style everything. Or Chandra Mythros? No, she was a bit too gothic, you were likely to return to massed outbreaks of bats and spiders. The African girl, Amari, was lovely. She drew with simplicity, and appreciated skies and colour, but she hadn't seen or heard from her in years. That was partly the pressure of work, which gave her no time to socialise, but she wasn't a people person anyway, she was content to just draw. She was an introvert and a recluse. If anybody ever wrote a book about her, that's probably how they would describe her.

She looked across at a little message frame that was etched into the wall above the table. On it were a few initials, written in circles, but not many, and they were all covered in a layer of dust. Some other Aylas had dozens of friends, some even had hundreds. She couldn't be bothered with that. When people came to visit, they sometimes wrote their initials in the frame so you could contact them again. There used to be a lot more, but she'd got fed up with having lots of 'friends' that she either didn't really want to see again, or who never bothered to visit. She had gone through them all one evening and rubbed a lot of them out. Starting with 'BG'.

Something rustled far down in the valley below. She instinctively turned her head towards the entrance, but it wasn't worth getting up to look. The auras of life forms were feint, and difficult to see in the daylight, that was why Aylas preferred to work at night. It would be one of those furry things with the big eyes and the curly tail, that liked to climb. There were few animals in this world, and no birds. She quite liked birds, most of her worlds had lots of different kinds of birds in them. It would be nice to have some here, but that would mean someone would have to add a template for them to its drawing, and she didn't know where that was, nor had she any way to find out.

In fact, she didn't even know who had created it. There was plenty of evidence that it once had human beings in it, but she'd never seen any, so the symbol for them had presumably been erased and they had all died out. Nothing new had appeared in this world during all the time she had been here, so maybe its Ayla didn't care about it anymore, or perhaps something had happened to her, and no-one was looking after it. If she could find its drawing, she would be able to spice it up a bit, but it could be anywhere. It wasn't etiquette for an Ayla to mess with someone else's worlds without permission, but you could if you wanted to. You just risked incurring their wrath if they ever found out. It might be worth it though, if it meant having some nice birds.

It was somehow very strange when you realised that worlds were just drawings on a surface, which came to life, but even more unsettling to think that she was in one, and had surfaces on which she drew other worlds.

Apart from the primary symbols that made basic forms, and the secondary template symbols that organised life, there was also another set of symbols. They didn't have a proper name and it was hard to get anyone to talk about them, so they were surrounded in mystery and legend. What they did was to create very specific life forms. Not just general kinds of four legged animals, or birds without wings, or human beings with no tail, but single unique life forms with very highly targeted characteristics.

If you drew one of them in a world, it gave that world the ability to contain one creature of that type.

The only one of those symbols that she knew much about was the symbol for an Ayla, but she'd never drawn one in any of her worlds.

She took a big breath, followed by an equally big sigh. Now it was time to go and tend to some more of her drawings. For all she knew there might be horrible things happening all over the place, worlds needing more or fewer types of vegetation or animals, worlds growing too big and colliding with each other, or proto-worlds that had developed new life and needed some direction. If she tried hard, she might get round the remainder of the collection today, and that would alleviate any urgent problems. Then she could have another good night's sleep, and maybe start to think about revisiting some of them to do a bit of sculpting and art tomorrow.

Then she remembered - candles! Yes, she needed to get more candles in. You couldn't do any work without light, and when she was rushing about yesterday she had noticed that a lot of the shelves in the tunnels were empty.

She lifted up a floorboard and pulled out a handful, which she put on the table. That would be enough for today, but there weren't many left.

There was no supply of candles in this world, she would have to travel to a world where they had nice ones and, er... steal some. It wasn't really stealing of course, because she had created all the worlds and she owned them, so any candles that were in them were hers anyway.

After pulling the creepers back down to keep the room cool and shady, she set off to resume work on her drawings in the tunnels.

As she passed by the table to collect the candles, something caught her eye. One of the circles in the message frame was glowing! How had she not seen that before? She peered at it carefully. The initials in it were 'AW'. It took her a while to associate that with a face. It was written in the top corner. Who had written 'AW' in the top corner of her message frame? Then she remembered – Alkira, the aboriginal girl! That was ages ago! Why on earth would Alkira want to speak to her now? Alkira had been a friend of her family for as long as she could remember, and looked after her drawings for a while when she had gone off to see what was happening in that strange world with lots of water. Too much water, as she recalled, with a bit of a grimace. She was thoroughly sick of water by the time she'd got back, and it had taken her nearly a week to get her hair straight. She had rubbed a lot of the squiggles out of the drawing for that world and let more greens and yellows and browns grow into it. Her world-building had improved no end since those early-days.

That meant she still owed Alkira a favour, of course, but she wasn't ready to start meeting up with people right now, she'd only just got back.

Reaching out towards the wall she paused for a moment. Accept or decline? Alkira's worlds were beautiful, and she would love to see more of them. It would probably do her good to meet someone who didn't want to kill her, so maybe this was a good chance to make contact again. She touched the initials gently with two fingers, gathered up her candles, and strode off into the depths of the tunnels.

5 - The Visitor

It was easy for her to remember where she had left off the night before. After all, you don't make it your life's work to draw worlds and then not remember where you've put them all.

She spent the morning in and out of the shorter dead-end tunnels at the back of the complex, and when she'd finished all of those, she devoted an hour or two to the central part of the complex, where there was a sort of hub with passages that went off in all directions like spokes of a wheel. That was where she had first started drawing, so the worlds there were bigger and more complex and needed more attention.

By what felt like teatime she had covered a lot more ground in the area, but she was feeling tired again. Curses to that stupid city full of machines and people, she thought. She had probably started making errors of judgement again by now. It was time to be heading back, for an early night if she had anything to do with it.

After adding a few more strokes of black to a particularly bleak and horrible looking world, she set off towards her little room, which was a good ten minutes' walk. Fortunately, she'd already dealt with all the drawings in the tunnels on the route back, so there would be no distractions on the way.

She whistled a little tune to raise her spirits a bit as she strode purposefully around the corners. Of course, she knew her way, without even thinking about it. She would never get lost in her own home.

When she turned a corner about halfway along one of the bigger tunnels, the outline of a figure was standing some way ahead of her in the gloom. It gave off a faint orange glow around its edges. That took her aback, and she stopped dead in her tracks. It was a long time since she'd seen the unmistakable signature of another creator. All life forms had coloured outlines, every Ayla could see them, but nothing else had any orange in its aura.

"Hello!" called a voice, cheerfully, and then a little more uncertainly, "Ayla Marlow? Thank you for inviting me!"

She looked up, momentarily startled, at the dark outline which was now rushing towards her topped by a mass of curly hair. After accepting the invitation earlier in the day she'd been half-expecting a visit, but most guests took their time to turn up. Alkira hadn't wasted any time, that was for sure.

"Jennifer, please!", she gushed awkwardly, striding towards the figure. "Call me Jennifer... everybody calls me Jennifer these days!"

That wasn't quite true. Unless three people counted as 'everybody'.

She had wanted to say, "What do you want?", but there were pleasantries to make before that. It wasn't polite just to rush in. The art of conversation had never been her strong point, but she always tried as best she could.

"Nice to see you again!" said Alkira, looking her up and down. "I didn't recognise you for a moment. You look... er... smaller than I remember."

"Yes," replied Jennifer uncertainly, now not being the best time to talk about the unfortunate circumstances that had led to that. "Nice to see you again too... What do you want?"

Alkira gave her a big smile, which threatened to split her face. "Ah! Always direct and to the point, that's what we like!"

"You found me then?"

"Well, you had to be here somewhere. I just came back to one of the parts of your home I remembered from last time I was here. You're not hard to find when you whistle," she said.

This was typical of conversations that took place between Aylas. Nobody really had anything to say, but it was rude not to speak.

They looked at each other awkwardly for a moment.

"Well, er... Tea or something?" said Jennifer eventually.

"Yes. That would be... nice," replied Alkira.

"Good. Then we'll go back to my room, and I'll see what I can do."

With the pleasantries taken care of, they shuffled off together along the tunnels to the little room overlooking the valley.

***

The table was only just big enough for two people, and a bit awkward if you wanted to put mugs of tea and your elbows on it as well. Having left the little kettle steaming gently all day there had only been enough hot water in it to make tea for one, so she had made herself something else.

Alkira waved her hand somewhat majestically in an arc through the air.

"I bring news from The Council!" she intoned.

Jennifer looked up suspiciously from her mug of cold liquid.

"Oh really!" she replied dryly, trying to sound interested, and failing. In her experience, news from The Council was probably not good news. It wasn't even really a proper council anyway, she thought. It was a group of people who had decided they were somehow better and more important than everyone else. If you agreed with that, you were sometimes reluctantly allowed to remain alive, and admit you were supposed to do what they said.

"Yes!" continued Alkira, with enthusiasm. "They're very impressed with your work here!"

She paused, waiting for the expression of delight to break across Jennifer's face.

Nothing happened.

"Oh good," replied Jennifer, weakly.

"Yes! They have seen how well you tend to your worlds, how much love you give to them, and how good you are at getting down and solving the problems you find in them," she continued, trying to read the expression that was looking back at her over the rim of the mug, "...and, they have a very special opportunity for you!"

"Oh, I see," replied Jennifer, thoughtfully. "You mean they're in trouble?"

Alkira paused. That was the problem when you wanted to recruit people who were cleverer than you were. You could never really get the better of them, because they were cleverer than you were.

"Er... well... yesss! There is something that you could help them with, but first," she replied, putting her outstretched hands on the table, "there are some secrets I need to tell you!"

Jennifer was now getting tired of a conversation where almost every sentence ended with an exclamation mark. She would have to think about this. The Council, from what she could recall, liked to sit around sipping fragrant tea from little cups, putting them on saucers with doilies, and nibbling on silly little macaroons and mille feuille, whilst indulging in polite conversation about trivia, and insulting each other.

It was perfectly plausible that they would want her to do something for them. They never actually seemed to achieve anything themselves, but it was easy to underestimate the degree of scheming and plotting and spitefulness that was at the heart of almost every committee, especially ones made up almost exclusively of old women. As far as she was aware, nobody had really seen much of her work here, but somehow it seemed her reputation had spread, which was odd. Probably her reputation for being hard working, hard headed, and for keeping herself to herself. That meant nobody would miss her, so she was expendable. She was also good at creating worlds and escaping death while doing dangerous things. That was exciting, if only a little bit. But did she want to do anything for The Council? No, not really, she was happy here. But secrets? That was interesting. Perhaps, she thought, the drains are blocked up again.

She was suddenly aware that Alkira was still looking at her with an air of great expectation. She was going to have to reply.

"Okay," she said, trying to be polite. "What do you want?"

They sat together at the table for a long time, and Alkira told her secrets.

Jennifer had thought they might be difficult to understand, but they weren't. They were very simple, but she knew that simple things could be very powerful or very worrying. These were both.

Alkira had started out by asking her what she knew about the third type of symbols, the tertiary ones. She had said "Not much", which was partly true, but if there was trouble she didn't want to admit exactly what she knew until she'd found out what it was. A tertiary symbol was used to place a specific entity in a world. She knew that.

There were lots of old stories about those symbols. Her father once had a book about them which he kept locked away. They were mysterious and somehow taboo. If you were to ask anyone for information, they would invariably look furtively to the left and right, as if checking that no-one was listening, before telling you that they knew nothing about them, and implying that you shouldn't either. But now here she was, sat at her little wooden table in the dying light of the day with an Ayla she hadn't seen for nearly a decade, talking about them quite openly in the same way that a parent might teach a child the alphabet.

There were quite a lot of them, but very few people knew exactly what most of them created, so it wasn't good to draw them, at least not in a world. Alkira borrowed a piece of charcoal and drew some of them on the otherwise featureless wall next to the table. It was alright if there was no life around them to make anything, you could draw them and rub them out again. No harm done. What you didn't want to do was to draw them in a world where life could gather around them and create something. That was true for the other more common template symbols as well. You could draw the template for a tree, but if there was no suitable life around it to create one it didn't do anything. It was the same with the symbol for an Ayla – which Alkira drew on her wall! Actually on her wall! She couldn't believe it. She knew what it looked like, but no-one would ever draw it. Some symbols you just didn't draw because, legend said, they gave rise to things that you really didn't want, and then you couldn't get rid of them. You could erase the symbol, of course, nothing was permanent, but what it had created didn't go away until it died, and that was a problem if it was immortal.

Jennifer sat, with her mug in her hands, listening to Alkira reciting her impromptu lecture on the subject of 'Tertiary Symbols and What You Shouldn't Know About Them'. She was nearly falling asleep by the time Alkira had reached the end of it. It didn't so much end as dribble off into nothingness.

"And so," said Alkira eventually, looking hard at the grubby little face that was still peering at her over the mug. "Are you willing to help us?"

Jennifer looked back at her through sleepy eyes.

"A reward!" added Alkira brightly, trying to generate some response. "Secrets of the tertiary symbols revealed?" she goaded.

"You've already told me about those now."

"Oh yes. So I have," said Alkira. "But you have to admit you're interested?"

The grubby hand put down the mug.

"Yes," she replied, "I have to admit that I am. But you still haven't told me exactly what it is that you want."

"Well, you have to help us," pleaded Alkira. "Something has started to destroy worlds, and nobody knows what it is."

Jennifer thought about this for a moment. Things often destroyed worlds. Usually it was the creatures that lived in them. Most creatures typically grew and developed alongside each other, forming a balance. Their growth, and therefore their ability to do serious damage, was limited by factors in the surrounding environment. It wasn't unusual however for some worlds to develop creatures that reproduced uncontrollably and threatened to destroy their entire existence. That wasn't what Alkira meant though, she was referring to something much more sinister. Jennifer had only just got back from one very emotionally and physically tiring expedition, and had been looking forward to spending some more time at home and unwinding, but she had to admit it sounded interesting.

"Okay," she said eventually. "You've got my attention, but I'm not promising anything."

Alkira seemed relieved.

"You must come with me and see for yourself," she said. "It's not something I can easily explain."

Jennifer closed her eyes and shook her head slowly.

"Okay," she said wearily. "Let's meet up tomorrow. We'll go and look at whatever you want, and then I'll see what I can do."

That seemed to make her friend uneasy.

"No, we have to go now," she said. "This is important. It's very dangerous and it has to be sorted out straight away. That's what The Council want."

"Mmmm," thought Jennifer. As far as she was concerned, what The Council wanted was most easily achieved with a wall, some blindfolds and a number of men with rifles. Alkira seemed worried. It wouldn't do any harm to go and take a look, she supposed.

And so it was that Alkira took her gently by the hand, and they walked together far enough up the tunnel for the remaining light of the day not to affect them. Jennifer knew how this bit worked, of course. When you went somewhere with another Ayla for the first time, you didn't know where you were going. You had to let them take you. She closed her eyes, kept hold of Alkira's hand, and opened them after a few seconds to find herself in a new world.

6 - Twisted Land

They were standing in the middle of a huge cavern cut into the side of a sandstone mountain. There appeared to be only one entrance which opened out onto a deep orange sunset and the yellow sands of a rolling desert. It was exactly how she would have expected Alkira to live. It could only be described by one word, and that was stunning.

"So, here we are!" said Alkira, in a voice which seemed to be seeking some form of encouraging response from her guest.

Jennifer had walked to the entrance, and was watching wisps of sand drift gently off the top of a few distant dunes. In many worlds she had visited, the warm desert winds carried faint smells of spices and flavours from distant cities, bringing memories of home and civilisation to the minds of weary travellers who crossed its many trading routes. They considered that to be beautiful. The breeze here brought no smells, no hint of its origins or the places it had been. No memories of its past, no plans for the future. Nothing, except gentle warmth. In many ways she considered that to be even more beautiful. She had no reply.

"I would offer you something to drink," said Alkira, "but we've drunk a lot in the last few hours, and I don't know about you, but I need a wee."

And, with that, she scuttled off outside, leaving Jennifer to enjoy the view.

Jennifer turned back into the cavern. She had been looking forward to seeing more of Alkira's collection of beautiful worlds, but what she saw on the walls wasn't what she had expected to find. There were a few patches of colour here and there, surrounded by a lot of other collections of symbols, almost all dark. Each little patch had its own symbol for earth, wind and fire and rock. You would never repeat them in the same drawing, there was no point, so they had clearly once been separate collections, but were now all smudged together into a blackened mess.

Where were all the works of art? All the beautiful patches of greens and blues and oranges that gave rise to the millions of life forms, the flowing waters, the sunsets, the perfect starry nights and the trees that rustled in the soft warm winds?

She sensed footsteps somewhere behind her.

"This is all one world now," said Alkira, spreading her hands out as if to encompass everything. "This is how we found them."

"It all looks... broken!" said Jennifer, carefully.

"Yes, it is," replied Alkira, sadly. Jennifer looked at her, in the way that a parent might comfort a worried child. "Oh, but these are not *my* worlds!" continued her friend reassuringly.

"Whose are they then?" asked Jennifer, feeling relieved but a bit confused.

"Nobody knows," replied Alkira. "Trouble was reported in a few worlds and The Council traced it back here. Something had been drawn in one of the pictures."

Jennifer just continued to look at her.

"And...?" she said.

"The symbol was a bow and arrow. It is supposed to generate a creature that hunts out trouble and makes life good."

"But you think it isn't doing what it's supposed to?" mused Jennifer thoughtfully.

"Well, maybe. We don't know. Over the next few days that world degenerated and turned into a patch of smudges." Jennifer looked more closely at the wall as Alkira continued. "Then it somehow moved across to the world next to it."

Jennifer raised her eyebrows at that. Travel between different worlds! Nothing she knew of could do that. Except an Ayla, of course.

"Okay, and... then that world died as well, and it moved on to another, and another..."

Alkira left the last sentence hanging.

"I see," replied Jennifer. Her mind was racing now. "Did anyone visit them to see exactly what was happening?"

"Well, yes," replied Alkira. "Apparently they were horrible. Things fighting and dying, and decay everywhere, and eventually most of the colours drained out of the worlds, and they grew bigger and er... sort of smudgy, and joined up with the ones around them."

"And this happened after the thing that was drawn moved between them?"

"Yes."

"Where is it now?"

Alkira just looked at her and shrugged.

"It's all one big mess now, most of the worlds overlap. It could be anywhere, but it's likely to be somewhere near its symbol," she said, indicating one of the few coloured patches that remained on the wall.

"And what do the council say about it?" asked Jennifer.

"They think it will keep moving around between worlds until it has fixed them all."

"Which means destroyed them all?" asked Jennifer rhetorically, as she ran her hands over the surface, examining various parts of it in more detail.

"Well possibly. But then no-one knows what it will do next. Some of the others think it might be able to jump to other worlds that are... er... drawn in other places..."

That stopped Jennifer in her tracks. She thought about it for a moment. That would be why The Council were worried. They might be a bit annoyed if something destroyed all someone's worlds, but if it could do what they thought, then it might be able to destroy *all* the worlds. All the worlds, everywhere.

"Oh shit," she said.

"Yes indeed... Lots of it... But we..." she corrected herself, "they, think it won't move anywhere else until it has finished here."

"Oh good," replied Jennifer, weakly. "Has anyone else been sent to look for it?"

"Yes," replied Alkira. "The council have even sent their warriors and bodyguards. Seven of them, in fact."

"And they didn't succeed," replied Jennifer quietly, more to herself than anyone else. "Why couldn't they sort it out? What was the problem? What did they have to say about it?"

"We don't know," replied Alkira, very sadly. "They never came back."

Jennifer was beginning to have sinking feelings about this.

"So, the council think *I* can do something about it. Strange. What did they tell you to tell me?"

"They said your mission would be to destroy it at all costs," replied Alkira, somewhat sternly.

Ayla Jennifer Marlow had never dealt directly with the council, but that sounded like an order from the leader, Number One, and she knew exactly what it meant. The expression 'at all costs' was the bit that worried her. It meant 'even if you don't come back'.

Jennifer turned towards the view of the rolling desert, and stood motionless in thought for what seemed like a very long time. It sounded like an adventure, that was for sure. Another tertiary creature that would probably be something like an Ayla, but not really, and which had the power to destroy worlds. Most of the creatures that she created seemed intelligent, but were really quite stupid really, she could generally outsmart them. This one might be different though. If it could destroy other creatures and worlds it sounded like it might the equivalent of an anti-Ayla. That was both interesting and worrying at the same time.

Alkira derailed her train of thought.

"If you want to help you should go now!" she said. "We don't know what else we can do, and everything's just getting worse. There may not be much time. I will look after your worlds for you while you are away."

Jennifer contemplated that, but only briefly. Was there any choice? No. Not really. If whatever-it-was could jump to worlds in other universes it could destroy the ones she had created as well. It could even destroy the one she was living in, so nothing and no-one was safe. Alkira would probably look after her drawings back home very well. And not put dangerous symbols in them either, she thought. But why had the council chosen her? She had seen some of the other people that the council had access to. They were formidable characters. Big, strong, you wouldn't want to trifle with them.

Alkira appeared to read her thoughts.

"The council don't think that brute force is the answer," she said quietly. "They think that sending someone who's... er... very clever, might do the trick."

It all made sense to Jennifer now.

"Ah, I see. When all else fails, send the geek."

"Well, no, not exactly," said Alkira quickly, trying to backtrack a bit. "It's just that..."

Jennifer waved her hand dismissively.

"Yes, I know. Don't worry, it's the truth." She took a big breath, followed by an equally big sigh.

"So... er... does that mean you'll go?" asked Alkira, wringing her hands, and looking hopeful. "Don't worry," she added. "I'll go straight back to your place, and stay there until you return, so if you come back... I mean... *when* you come back, just go home, and I'll be there. I can't tell you much more to help, unfortunately. You're on your own now, as they say." She looked across to Jennifer who now studying the smudged patches carefully again, but there was no response. "Do you think you can remember it all?"

Jennifer nodded slowly. She was sure she could remember enough of it. There would be some strange life-forms, she thought, and some of it looked very odd, but dealing with that was part of being a creator. The best part about agreeing to go would be that she could get away from what was turning out to be an increasingly awkward conversation.

After another moment or two she reached out, as if to take Alkira's hand, before having an important thought. She ran off to the cave opening, where she paused to memorise the view. Then she picked up a small stick that was lying on the ground, and placed it at an angle against the wall, just inside the cave. That would do, she thought. She ran back to Alkira, took her hand and closed her eyes. Nothing needed to be said, every Ayla knew what that meant. It meant, "Let's go".

After two or three steps she felt Alkira release her hand, and she opened her eyes in the dim light of another world.

It appeared to be late evening here.

"So where do I... start..." she said, turning round.

No-one was there.

"Ah!" she thought. Clearly, Alkira wasn't staying. She had been 'dropped off', a bit like a guest that you're glad to get rid of, and now it was up to her to make her own way.

After her eyes had adjusted to the dim light, she was able to see the surroundings a little better. It was indeed a strange world, that was for sure. This bit of it wasn't destroyed by any means. Lots of green, but there were hills everywhere. The green she could appreciate, she did that too in her drawings, however the rest of the world looked like it was going to be a proper challenge. It was getting darker by the minute, but she could make out a forest to her right, with shapes that could be a city on the distant horizon, and a river to her left.

The comfort of home had been short-lived, she thought. After spending all that time in the dirty city she'd been looking forward to a few days' rest, but now everything had changed yet again, and she was on another mission.

No-one had any idea what kind of creature the symbol would have created, but there was only one way to find out. She turned downhill toward the gloomy forest. That would be the best place for something to hide.

It was time to go back into the darkness.

7 - The Seat of Trouble

There are not many places, in any realm, where a typical secret society can find a meeting hall that lives up to expectations. When you're a group of creatures who create worlds and can travel to any place and time you like, you would think that the task would become a bit easier, but it's a universal truth that some people are just incapable of being happy unless they have something to complain about.

This secret society didn't have a name because nobody needed to talk about it. It was simply called The Council.

A shaft of moonlight sloped through an opening in the vaulted roof and fell across a little circular table, but was lost amongst the yellow and orange glow from the electric chandelier which hung from the centre of the ceiling. On the table was a cloth shaped in the form of a star with a number on each of the six points, which draped over the edge like the wilted petals of a dying flower. The centre of the table was stacked with a formidable mass of cake stands and teapots. Eight places for afternoon tea were squeezed around the edge, so few of them matched up with one of the six points.

Around it sat seven figures, four of them wearing shabby theatrical masques. In the background, the outline of an old man carrying an empty tray was disappearing through an elegant arched doorway into the bowels of the building.

"Ooh, you must try one of these!" squealed one of the voices. It belonged to a thin lady in a white dress who was occupying the fourth chair.

"Mmmm, what is it Number Three?" replied Number Two,

"It's one of those – things – there with the pink icing!"

Long thin fingers reached out.

"That's the last one of those. I wanted that!" complained the figure sat at the sixth chair around the table, trying to sound offended.

"Yes, Number Four," intoned Number Five, who was, against all expectations, sitting in the eighth seat, "...but these flaky pastry tarts over here are just as nice!"

"JEFFERSON!" shouted a voice.

"Oh dear, this is terribly confusing, isn't it?" wailed Number Four, looking across at Number Three, who was two places away from her.

"Not really," said Number Two.

"Well, not for you, because you're sat in the right place!" replied Number Five.

"Ah well, yes. Number One and I decided that, with three guests this evening we would space ourselves out round the table, sort of, interleave them, so that they felt *included* so to speak," she said, attempting to make the word *included* sound as if it meant something special.

Number Four pulled a funny face. Being interleaved with people wasn't something she approved of. Even if they were other Aylas. Of course, all Aylas were equal, but some were just better than others.

"Anyway," she proclaimed, "where is Number One? She's late!"

The old man had appeared from the doorway and was shuffling across the floor towards the assembled figures. He was a stocky little man, with grey hair and spectacles, and carried a white towel over his arm.

"More of those pink things!" shouted Number Three at him as he approached.

"Yes Ma'am. I'll check Ma'am," intoned the figure, before turning around slowly and making his way back towards the door again.

There was a general mutter of disapproval, interrupted by Number Two.

"Never fear Number Six, Number One will be here shortly," she said somewhat uncertainly. "She's just delayed momentarily."

"I'm Number Four! Number Six isn't here."

"Ah, yes. Sorry about that."

"Well, I thought you said that you weren't confused."

"I'm not!"

"But the six of us have been meeting around this table for years," squeaked Number Four irritably, "and I'm the only one of us with red hair. You can see bits of it sticking out quite clearly!", she added, tugging at an errant curl.

"Yes," replied Number Two, frustrated, "but that's not the point," she whispered loudly. "We use our numbers so that nobody knows who we really are. You know that!"

Number Four did know that. She also knew that everybody sat around the table knew very well who each other were. Even the three guests sat around the table knew who everybody was, there wasn't any point in trying to disguise it, but if The Council didn't call themselves a *secret* society they would just be a society, and that didn't sound very imposing. Besides, it was always nice to pretend anonymity, because then you could offend people, and nobody knew who you were.

Jefferson re-appeared from the doorway with a plate on his tray containing three pink cakes, which he placed on the table.

"Is that all you've got?" snapped Number Three.

"Apologies Ma'am."

"Pah!" she said dismissively. "You know we like those. Get more next time!"

"Yes Ma'am. Apologies Ma'am," said the man quietly, before turning to leave.

"I should think so," growled Number Three at his departing shape.

"And where is Number Six, there isn't even a place set for her?"

Number Two looked across briefly at the numeral on the tablecloth, before settling her gaze back on Number Four. Number Six was usually the last place on the circular table setting, to the right of Number One, and she was Number One's right-hand woman, both on the seating plan and literally. Number Two sat to the left of Number One and was sometimes referred to as her left-hand woman. She had never really understood the merit of that, or been especially pleased about the idea. It didn't seem to have a particularly credible ring about it, however it did mean that, right at this moment, she was probably in charge.

"Number Six is... otherwise indisposed tonight," she said, maintaining the eye contact, but with a tinge of uncertainty in her voice. "She is away on business, so tonight there will only be five of us."

"Eight of us," corrected Number Four, irritably. She was still not really happy with the idea of being *interleaved*, and besides, there wasn't enough room for her elbows, which made it difficult to hold her cup of tea and eat her mille feuille at the same time.

Away towards the back of the hall, the clattering of the entrance door momentarily interrupted the proceedings and, a moment later a tall thin figure dressed in a dark robe came striding across the floor towards the group, clutching what appeared to be a substantial folder of papers.

She cleared away a sprinkling of macaroon crumbs from the tablecloth in front of her seat with a sweep of her hand and dropped the folder on the table with a *thud*, causing the cake stands to rattle, accompanied by an assortment of tinkles from various cups and spoons.

"Right then," she said sternly, drawing herself up to her full height. "Let's begin. We have a very packed agenda this afternoon."

Number Five had been considering the seating arrangements and had realised that, in the absence of Number Six and the addition of the extra places, she was sat directly on the right of Number One, which made her Number One's right-hand woman! At least logically anyway. She peered up expectantly at Number One with a little simpering smile in anticipation of the eye contact which usually conveyed the unspoken recognition between the chief and her immediate deputy.

Number One ignored her.

"Firstly, it is very rare that we are honoured by guests at one of our meetings," she began, "however this afternoon is a special occasion because we are joined by..."

Her attention was drawn to the top of a head, whose face was peering intently into a cup. "Are you with us, Number Four?" she enquired, somewhat abruptly.

"I've got crumbs in my tea."

Number One looked down at her with an expression that was a mixture of frustration and patience. It was always like this, she thought. They were blessed with a very short attention span, and little intelligence, but that was good for a leader. At least it allowed her the freedom to do pretty much whatever she wanted provided she maintained the illusion of democracy.

"Fish them out with your spoon!" squeaked Number Three.

"She doesn't have one," said Number Five.

"Why not?"

"Because she doesn't take sugar and..."

"But she does put milk in it!" interrupted Number Two.

"Yes, but not a lot because she drinks Earl Grey and you only put a little spot in. It mixes up by itself. You don't have to stir it."

"You could try a table napkin!" said Number Five, helpfully. "If you twizzle up the corner you can sometimes wick them out!".

"Oh no. It's alright," said Number Four, "It doesn't matter now anyway because they've sunk."

"THIS AFTERNOON IS A SPECIAL OCCASION..." repeated Number one, sternly, "...because we are joined by three very good friends of ours, who may well be able to shed some light on this ongoing situation which has been causing us all a serious problem for a long time now and which, if it is allowed to continue, could result in the end of civilisation as we know it."

"It tastes funny now," muttered Number Four.

Number One paused until she had managed to make eye contact with each of the other members with a carefully practised dagger-like gaze that conveyed the contemplation of unspeakable threats being formed ready to unleash on the perpetrator of any further disturbance.

"So... if I may have your undivided attention to the matters in hand, I would like to commence the evening's proceedings by introducing our guests. Please make them feel welcome, Ayla Mubara, Ayla Goodison, and Ayla Mythros."

There followed a muttering of unintelligible noises, from the assemblage of old women.

Number One opened the folder and shuffled through the tatty documents, arranging a few of them in front of her on the table, and moving others to the front of the stack.

"Now," she continued, which silenced the hubbub. "The first order of the afternoon. It appears that considerable progress has been made in our quest to recruit a replacement agent..."

"Yet another replacement agent," interrupted Number Two despondently.

Number One fixed her with the disapproving stare, before turning her gaze back to the document.

"A REPLACEMENT AGENT…" she continued pointedly, "…to investigate and remedy this very awkward situation that has arisen due to the unauthorised creation of this *bow-and-arrow* creature."

Several faces turned away, seemingly to pay an unusual amount of attention to their cups of tea.

"As you will all have seen, the situation is becoming serious and there may not be time for another attempt. So…" she continued, "I have had no choice but to take the advice of our esteemed guests under advisement. Their recommendation seems to me to be utterly ridiculous, but I am assured that the choice will be a good one. Convince me then," she said, gathering a deep breath. "What do we know about this *Jennifer Marlow*…"

8 - Back in the Forest

...who was currently standing amongst the trees on the side of a cold wet hillside in the rain, wondering why she had ever thought it would be a good idea to get out of bed that morning.

When a world gets angry it usually takes out its frustrations by raining on everybody, or at least that's what Jennifer had observed over many years of travelling. This world didn't seem to be any different. The rain was just relentless tonight. It felt as if it was running down the back of her neck and warming itself up somewhere around her waist, before soaking down her legs and dribbling into her socks, where it proceeded to escape by bubbling out over the sides of her shoes with each step she took. She certainly wouldn't be needing to wash her hair for a day or two, assuming of course she was ever able to get it dry again. At least her feet weren't cold because her shoes were full of warm water, which was something in the way of a consolation.

She'd moved carefully downhill between the trees towards the river on an animal track, but hadn't really travelled very far. Based on what she had seen and felt, this was the right place. The strange creature should be here somewhere. She looked around through the streaks of falling rain, but it was hard to see anything except darkness. That was the problem with the inhabitants of these worlds, she thought. Most people would have said they couldn't see *anything*, but that simply wasn't true, they could see lots of darkness, but they didn't consider the darkness to be important. They referred to it as *nothing*. They didn't like abstract concepts much.

The first thing she had to do was to try and understand exactly where she was.

Just then, something caught her eye. An object with red and white lights on it was flickering through the trees in the distance. It looked as if a motorised vehicle of some sort was winding its way down a road on the side of another hill. She watched it for a few moments until it disappeared from view, presumably into a valley.

That meant this was a time and place where there were people and machines. As far as she could tell, people and machines didn't manage to exist for a very long time in any world, but wherever they did exist there was always trouble, she thought.

The world seemed to agree, it rained a bit harder.

Now that her eyes were becoming more accustomed to the surroundings, she was able to see other things more clearly. A few hundred yards away to her left, a couple of creatures were moving cautiously along the ground. Things with four legs and a tail, but only one head she noted with some relief. She recognised their auras. Most civilisations knew them as some form of 'dog' or 'wolf'. That was what everyone drew templates for these days. Four-legged dogs with one head were *in vogue*. The old experimental idea of drawing templates for dogs with multiple heads was now consigned to history. Those silly ideas had died out even before she had started drawing worlds. Someone who thought they were being clever once had a great idea that a big, fierce, three headed dog would be a fantastic, invincible guardian because an attacker could only fight one head at a time, and one of the other two heads would eat him. It hadn't taken most intelligent civilisations long to realise that all they had to do to defeat it was to send three people.

Looking upwards she could see that lots of other creatures were sitting in the tops of the trees. Not moving. Some of them would be birds of course, she noted with a tinge of sadness. They were warm, and alive. She could sense their faint coloured outlines in the darkness. Tucked up and asleep with not a care in the world, while the wind and rain lashed around them. Like I should be, she thought, snuggled in my little bed. A big dribble of cold rain trickled down her back. "Yes. I know you're not pleased," she whispered. "But don't take it out on me, I'm not responsible for your problems. You're not my world, I didn't draw you. I'm just trying to help."

This was where Alkira believed the creature was living at the moment. While they were looking at the drawing in the cave they had talked about its apparent behaviour, and from what she understood, it was territorial. It tended to stay in one area for long periods of time, only moving on when it had destroyed everything. Alkira said its symbol had last been seen in the drawing for this world, which was one of the patches on the wall that still had any colour left in it. Assuming she was correct, there was every chance it was nearby because it wasn't a very big world.

If it really was a hunter, it would have a very sharp sense of awareness, and well-honed tracking skills. On the face of it, a bow and arrow didn't sound like a very formidable weapon, but she didn't fancy contemplating the truth of that when she had a spike sticking out of her back.

There was no way it could know she was here yet, so it wouldn't be actively looking for her. The best thing she could do would be to keep quiet and wait. Sitting down wasn't the best idea, it would only increase her response time if she needed to run, so there wasn't any option other than to stand in the rain and watch, very carefully. There were two larger trees quite close together a couple of steps off the track. She moved silently into the shadows between them and tried not to exist. The outline of her shape, already faint, began to merge with the darkness of the background until, after a few seconds, nothing appeared to exist there at all. If an onlooker were to peer into the gloom carefully enough, they might notice that some patches of the blackness seemed to be a bit darker than others, but on the whole, they would conclude very firmly that there was nothing there.

After scanning the surroundings for a while, her attention was drawn to a rustling noise which came from some distance away on her left. Standing on the path was a creature with a human-sized outline, but it wasn't a human being. It was different. The eye was drawn to it. Its outline was coloured, like other life that had been formed around a template, but there was a tinge of red, or orange to it. For a moment she was taken aback. What sort of life gathered around a template to make something with a red edge? True, it had the other colours normally associated with constructed life forms, blues and greens and yellows, but mixed in with this outline were little threads of orange and red.

"That must be it!" she thought. "There's nothing else it could be."

After remaining stationary for a moment or two, it set off slowly along the path towards her, pausing a few steps in front of the trees where she was standing and looking around cautiously, but without noticing her.

She followed it, keeping her distance. No matter how quietly she moved it seemed to hear her, or it thought it heard *something*, because it would stop and look back. Occasionally it would even turn around and walk back towards her for a better look, and she would have to hide in the shadows. It never saw anything, of course, because she could simply disappear if she wanted, but that was annoying. Disappearing didn't take any physical effort, but after a while the concentration needed to do it made her brain hurt, so it wasn't something that she did unless she absolutely had to. The problem with following this thing was that it seemed to be aware of her all the time, whenever she moved. Most life forms weren't that perceptive.

She let it get further ahead, and then faded into the shadows near a tree, re-emerging a few seconds later from a dark patch a bit further up the path. That had worked. It hadn't noticed. So, it only knew she was there when she moved and made noise, not when she disappeared and came back in a different place. It couldn't detect that, which gave her an advantage.

She waited until there were a few dozen paces or so between them, and then repeated the process, appearing faintly in a patch of trees a few yards from the path in a position where she could see it. The shape didn't turn to look, but it did seem to be on edge. It wasn't moving as fluently as it had been. Maybe it didn't hear any noise, but it seemed to know that something wasn't right.

Now she was in a position to observe it better. So, it was a human! Well, human shaped anyway. It had been walking like one and she'd not seen it use anything except two legs. It paused on the path, almost directly in line of sight, and took something from its shoulder. It then produced a stick from a bag on its back.

"Ah yes!" she thought. "It *is* a human after all, and this is what a bow and arrow symbol creates. It's a hunter of some sort!"

After tracking it for what seemed like ages, she had made up her mind. It was definitely a human male. It had managed to kill a few creatures with its weapon, mostly things that lived up in the trees, but it had shot a rabbit as well. Now it seemed like it was heading back to wherever it called home. Her brain hurt, but she was going to have to keep up with it.

She continued to follow at a distance, being careful not to lose sight of it, until it finally disappeared around a corner of a dense clump of trees.

When she arrived at the corner it was apparent that the path ended at the edge of a road, and seemed to pick up again at the other side. There was a wide gap in the trees where the ground was well trodden. Animals probably used it as a track through the forest, she thought. Stopping abruptly at the edge of the wet, black tarmac she looked around. The figure was nowhere to be seen.

She ran across to the gap in the trees at the other side and peered down into the darkness. The ground sloped away towards a rocky ledge, and was littered with sharp boulders. He wasn't anywhere in sight, but apart from the trees either side which had no apparent path through them, there was nowhere he could have gone. This wasn't good! She was now beginning to get worried. It was something that she knew very well was a bad idea. All the rules said whatever you do don't panic, because when you panic you get lost.

She ran back across the road to the place where she had seen him last, and looked around. Yes, of course, they all knew he could move between worlds, that was why she was here, but it wasn't obvious whether he could just do it at will, like she could!

When an Ayla moves between worlds there's a momentary trace. There's a mark in the fabric of the world they've left, like the dent that remains on a piece of paper when an artist has drawn something on the top sheet of a pad and then torn it off, exposing a blank piece of paper underneath with faint indentations on it. But here there was nothing, so she had lost him! All that work, all that time. If she couldn't see where he had gone, all the effort of the evening was wasted and it might take days or weeks before he returned to this area again, if ever.

Maybe there was something she had missed? Maybe there was somewhere to go, and she just hadn't seen it? This was frustrating. She turned, and began to run back across towards the gap in the trees at the other side. After taking two steps into the road, she was suddenly aware of a sound coming from her right, which startled her, so she stopped and turned.

What happened next was something that would etch itself into her memory and stay there for the rest of her life.

She heard the unmistakable noise of an engine, then a monster with two giant yellow eyes appeared from around the corner, racing towards her with a deafening roar!

The best thing to do would have been to step sideways. Either way would have done, back to the edge she had just stepped away from, or across to the other side.

The second-best thing would have been to simply vanish into the darkness.

It was always easy to say that in retrospect.

She was hungry, she was cold, she was tired, and she had a headache from disappearing so often. By the time her brain had contemplated any of this it was too late. The yellow headlamps burned patterns into the back of her eyes as they came ever closer, but despite this she could see every detail very clearly.

Little wipers flopped erratically across the windscreen, and raindrops sparkled in the headlight beams. Darkness and silence were always the ideal conditions for travelling between worlds. Confusion, bright lights and noise were not the best. She tried to imagine another world. Home would do. Anywhere would do, but there was nowhere at home quite like this, and few places she could think of in any other world that were similar enough that she could get her pounding head and tired body to believe that this place could be anything like them. She'd been to something called a *nightclub* once with searchlights and trance music which she could imagine sounded a bit like the engine, and she was tired then too. She just had to convince herself that she was there, and not here. For a fleeting moment she believed she might have managed it. The world went quieter, time seemed to slow down, and the looming vehicle began to develop translucent patches as it raced towards her. Some of the rain stopped landing on her, and the world began to feel warmer.

Then she noticed. There were two figures in the car, the driver was looking across to a smaller figure in the passenger seat. He appeared to be talking to it. She focused harder on the occupants. It looked like a child. Then the driver looked back up at the road, to see the ghostly apparition of a young girl, with sparkling drops of rain blowing through her body, standing, or floating, right in his path. She looked straight at him and realised that her plan wasn't going to work, she'd been distracted too long and there wasn't time to re-focus her mind. There would still have been time to jump out of the way, but she wasn't stood on ground that existed in any one world anymore, and there simply wasn't any way to move.

Then the car began to swerve. The driver struggled briefly with the controls. It slid sideways and there was an enormous crash and a bump as it hit one of the boulders at the side of the road and two of the wheels went onto the dirt. Glancing sideways, she saw the red tail lights disappear down the embankment, in the gap between the trees towards the rocky ledge.

She abandoned the effort of trying to move between worlds, and once her feet were back on solid ground, ran across to investigate.

The car must have hit something because it was rolling over and over. The figures inside it seemed to be normal human life forms with the usual-coloured outlines. In the darkness every living thing had a pattern, she saw them all the time and she knew instinctively that one of the shapes was female and one was male. From the look of it the female one was the younger of the two, it was hard to tell when they were being thrown around so much. She watched as the car disappeared over the edge of the rocky outcrop. Headlights flickered upwards through the falling rain, and there was a soft splash before the world slowly returned to quietness, punctuated only by the sound of the rain on the leaves.

9 - Rescue

On the ground, about halfway down the embankment where the car had rolled over and over, was an outline. It wasn't moving. The younger human, the girl, had been thrown out before the car had plunged over the edge.

"Okay," said Jennifer, taking a big breath and pulling her soaking clothes around herself a bit more tightly. "I got away with that! Now what?" That was the point at which she realised that she was shivering, and talking to herself.
She looked around again. There was still no trace of the bow-and-arrow man. There was plenty of life, but nothing with the remotest bit of red in its outline.

He'd got away, and there was really nothing more she could do tonight.

She would need to find somewhere warm and dry, where there was a comfortable place to rest and where there would be food. Somewhere that wouldn't take too much mental effort to get to, because really honestly, her brain felt like a bag of jellyfish now.

She turned once again to scan the surroundings, in the vain hope that there might be something she had missed.

No, nothing. Her gaze fell back to the girl on the ground. She was still alive but hadn't moved. She wasn't going to be any help, and she would die soon anyway in this weather.

In response to this thought the world rained on the top of her head a little bit harder.

"What?" she said, annoyed. "This is nothing to do with me!"

That was true really. It wasn't anything to do with her. People had accidents and died all the time. People were a commodity, like candles. The world just made new ones. You made them, you burnt them, they gave you light, you enjoyed them, but one day they just became a useless stub, and you threw them away.

She'd killed lots of people, usually when she'd had no choice, but sometimes because that was what she had to do, and always because they deserved it. Whatever that meant.

Despite this, something chafed her conscience.

Killing something felt different to just leaving something to die, especially when there wasn't any reason to want it dead. The problem was that, at this moment, she was having enough trouble keeping herself alive, never mind rescuing someone else. Another cold trickle of water ran down her back.

"Oh, alright then," she snapped. "I'll see what I can do."

It was a tricky and slippery route down the embankment to the unconscious girl, and difficult to pick a way through undergrowth and boulders, but eventually Jennifer reached her.

She was still alive, it looked like she had just hit her head. There was a bit of blood but nothing serious. To get her rescued, someone would have to find her because there was no way Jennifer could pick her up and carry her, and the ground was far too rough to drag her up to the side of the road where she might be found by another passing motorist, even if there was going to be one. No other cars had passed by in all the time she had been in the forest. If she wasn't careful there would be two people needing rescued.

In a remote spot like this it was a serious challenge.

If she couldn't move the girl, she'd have to move the world.

She went and sat on the edge of the rocky outcrop. Below her was the river, she could hear it. That would be where the car had gone, she thought, into the river. Nothing would have survived that.

There was no sign of any towns or villages in the landscape that was laid out before her, so she would have to find some.

She closed her eyes. That was the easy part. Closing them and staying awake was the hard part. It would have to be some time in the past. Trying to see the future caused all sorts of problems, but not the ones that people usually imagined. She opened her eyes and began to drift through the past. The sky flickered as the surroundings moved from year to year, decade to decade, century to century.

Sitting and watching time go by wasn't particularly strenuous, in fact it was quite relaxing really. Much easier than having to move physical things to different places. At least time didn't weigh anything.

Flickering through the past revealed a point in time where the river was flowing through a plain, further away from the hills. After a few minutes she decided on a particular scene which looked hopeful. The side of the hill was not so steep, and the ground sloped away more gently towards several settlements on a big wide plain. She moved back and forward a few years either side of her chosen time. The settlers went exploring and hunting in the evenings, and at night. It wasn't possible to see individuals at this distance, but on the whole, they seemed to have a stable and productive way of life. She hadn't seen any of the settlements attack each other, at least in the twenty or so years either side of her proposed time, so that was good too. After a little bit of fine-tuning, she found an evening where a small group of hunters were leaving a settlement and heading in her direction just as it was beginning to get dark. That was perfect.

Now for the hard bit. She would need to remember the place and time that she saw in front of her very accurately, so she sat and studied it. The snake of the river, the size and position of the forests, the placement of the huts and buildings in the settlements. She built a picture in her mind. The features on the horizon, the columns of smoke that drifted upwards from the glowing fires. Now the clouds and the sky, the smell of the air and the noises of the forest.

She closed her eyes. Back to the future then, a very wet place and time which she remembered well because she had just come from there.

Further up the embankment the unconscious girl was still alive, but getting colder in the rain. Her aura was getting fainter. Picking up the girl's hand she closed her eyes again. Now where did she want to be? She cleared her mind. Ah yes, the river looks like *this*, and the big wide plain has forests *here* and *here*, one is shaped a bit like an egg, and there are settlements *there* and *there*...

After a moment or two she had rebuilt the scene in her mind, with the glowing fires and the columns of smoke in exactly the right places. It was just like painting a picture from memory. There was enough detail in the mental image, there could be no other place and time that looked like this, especially when the sky and clouds were added to the picture, and the little group of settlers were walking up the hill towards them. That marked the place and time very well. She opened her eyes again. They were *somewhere* different because it wasn't raining anymore and stars were visible between a few thinning clouds, with a sliver of yellow crescent moon just above the horizon, which was exactly what she had wanted to see.

The girl was here with her, and so were a couple of the boulders which had come for the ride and seemed out of place now in this different world. A bit of overspill was unavoidable though, you couldn't choose exactly what to put your bubble around, sometimes you just had to take whatever you had hold of and drag it with you.

The surroundings looked right, which was a relief because, if they hadn't, she'd have had to do it again, and that might have meant taking them back to where they were before and starting from scratch. She walked down the embankment to the rocky ledge. Yes! The group of settlers were there. Now to get them up here, and hope that a strange unconscious girl was some use to them.

Jennifer crept down the side of the hill towards the figures, trying not to be seen or heard. She had no way of knowing how good they were at hunting, so she didn't know how quiet and clever she would have to be. There was no obvious path up the hill, once out of the forest it was just featureless scrub. She was able to get quite close to them undetected by treading carefully. They were a family. Human beings, slightly different colours to their outlines than the ones she had been seeing in the other place and time, but definitely human beings. Two adults and a young male. The boy had some kind of torch which he kept lit all the time. That appeared to be his purpose.

They didn't seem to be interested in climbing the steep side of the hill though, they were more intent on heading for the smaller of the two nearby forests. She picked up a twig and snapped it. That made the larger of the adults turn in her direction and look. Her jellyfish brain was not in the mood for disappearing into shadows, but she felt sure she was fairly well hidden. As she had hoped, they thought the noises were caused by an animal, and decided to stalk her. By rustling bits of foliage now and again and stepping judiciously on the occasional stick, she managed to lead them to within striking distance of the unconscious girl.

On seeing her they appeared to be interested. This was the moment of truth. Did they want another member for their settlement, or were they all too hungry? Was it worth their while to take an injured creature for any purpose other than to eat it? Jennifer watched intently from the cover of a clump of trees. They were picking her up, and they hadn't killed her first, which is probably what they would have done if she was destined to be food. She allowed herself an almost inaudible gasp. It was working!

She watched as the two adults carried the girl down the hillside, led by the boy with his burning torch. When they had become a dot in the darkness she allowed herself a big breath, followed by an equally big sigh. That was the best she could have done. She'd already been very tired and very hungry when she started, but now she also had to find her way back from a strange place and time to the world where she was hunting for the bow-and-arrow man, before her muddled brain forgot enough of the details to make the job of finding it impossible.

Fortunately, or unfortunately, the image of standing in the middle of a road about to be run down by a roaring metal monster with big yellow eyes, and not being able to move, was something her mind could recreate very easily. In fact, it was not something she was ever likely to forget.

She returned to the place and time shortly after the accident without much difficulty, and found a tree with a hollow amongst its big roots which was big enough to sit down and sleep in.

It wasn't very comfortable, and she still hadn't found any food, but it kept the rain off her, and it reminded her of home. Falling asleep was easy.

And now she was walking... well she was moving, but her feet weren't touching the ground. She was still in the forest, but the rain had stopped, and she felt a bit warmer. It wasn't completely dark either, which was odd. Moonlight sparkled off the leaves that dangled from overhanging branches as she pushed her way through them. They didn't seem to touch her. She emerged at the edge of a rocky outcrop and looked out across the dark landscape below.

A hand came up to her face... but this wasn't right. This wasn't her hand, and her face certainly didn't feel like this. Something was very wrong. She was looking down into the darkness at the faint outline of the river below. In the middle distance was the plain and the settlements, and figures climbing the hillside in a little pool of orange glow. As they approached it was apparent that they were hunters. Three of them, two adults and a boy. They reached the top of the embankment. She withdrew into the shadow of the trees. The two adult figures knelt in the grass by the unconscious girl, and one of them picked up her wrist. Then they looked at each other and nodded, before lifting her up by the arms and legs and starting to make their way over the ledge and back down into the valley.

Her head turned towards the tiniest noise. It came from the trees just across from where the girl had been laying. Her eyes scanned the shadows, but nothing seemed to be there. No outline, no aura, not even the faintest one. No creature. She walked to the edge of the rocky outcrop and watched. The little orange glow of the flame began to recede into the distance, becoming smaller and fainter.

And then she was off! Over the edge with an athletic but well calculated little jump, landing on the damp grass without skidding, and then away, down the side of the hill towards the plain. Moving quickly, her feet making no noise as she headed off in the direction of the little group. It felt... exciting!

Jennifer awoke from her dream with a start. Her arms and legs felt warmer, but her feet were still wet. There was sunshine through a canopy of bright green leaves, which made her blink until her eyes got used to the surroundings.

Slowly, she unfolded herself from the hollow in the roots of the tree and gave herself an experimental stretch. She had expected to find her body a wreck after the events of the night before. It was a bit aching and stiff, but everything seemed to still work. Looking around with the advantage of daylight she could make more sense of the surroundings.

The rocky ledge was nearer than she had imagined it would be, and the path up towards the road didn't look anywhere near as long and treacherous as it had seemed when she'd tackled it the evening before. When the world was dark and cold and wet, everything seemed further away, and harder, and if you weren't careful, you could easily become despondent. However, when the world was warm and the sun was shining, life seemed better and things were easier to do. She'd been around long enough to know that the trick to survival and success was to work smart. People gave up when they were tired and making no progress with their goals. The trick wasn't to give up, the trick was to rest, and the best time to rest was on the bad days when it was difficult to do things. That meant you were refreshed for working on the good days when things were easier to achieve. It was a lifestyle she had developed, and it usually worked. Except, that is, when the world decides you're going to save everyone from a bow-and-arrow man, and rescue a girl after crashing her car and nearly killing her.

Then she remembered the dream. Well, that was odd! A new experience. As far as she knew, she didn't dream very often and that had been a very strange one. Perhaps it was just a combination of being cold, wet, tired, hungry and in a different world? Maybe. She'd been cold, wet, tired and hungry in lots of different worlds, but never had a dream like that.

Anyway, this task was different, so what you had to do was adapt. There was little she could do to track the creature in the daylight, it would have to wait until tonight, so she would use the nice sunny day for a rest. Why not?

She climbed up the little steep path and paused at the edge of the road to look down. It was clear where the car had gone. There were skid marks on the road and wheel marks in the mud where it had slid sideways. One big boulder had paint marks and a lump knocked out of it, where the car must have hit it and rolled over, and there were bits of broken plastic and little nubs of broken glass everywhere. A few splintered saplings, and gouges out of the earth marked the path it had taken to the rocky outcrop, and over the edge on the way to its free fall down into the river.

"Oh well!" she said to herself, "At least the girl should be alright," before turning her face towards the sky, as if inviting the world to confirm that her actions had met with its approval. After the terrible rain and wind of the night before, it really was a nice day. Perhaps that was the answer she was looking for.

And she was hungry.

Around the corner, just along the road from the track she had come down the night before, was a junction with a signpost. In English it read 'Upper Spring'. Jennifer lived in a world of symbols, she couldn't read the writing in this world very well at all, but she knew it was a signpost that pointed to a town and, in her experience, most towns in the countryside in most worlds had food, usually in the form of something they called tea rooms or diners, so that was where she would go today. The walk would do her good, and it would be an adventure.

10 - The Tea Room

The walk up the road in the sunshine to the town at Upper Spring had been pleasant. Several cars had passed by her uneventfully, and nothing had tried to run her over.

There had indeed been a tea room, and she had found a quiet table near the window, where she could watch the world go by.

A lady in an apron holding a pad and pencil was standing in front of her, waiting for her order.

"Er, a pot of tea and a piece of cake please."

"What sort of cake?"

"Umm... I don't know. What have you got?"

The lady in the apron stuck her pen behind her ear, and pulled a small menu from the slot in a piece of wood that was sat in the middle of the table, which she put down for Jennifer to read. Jennifer squinted at the unintelligible marks and made a few peculiar faces.

"There's Victoria Sponge," proclaimed the lady, sensing her difficulty with what she imagined ought to be a simple decision, "or Coffee Cake, Banana Cake, Carrot Cake, or..." she continued, "our speciality is Eccles Cake. That's very nice."

Jennifer knew about lots of different cakes, they all sounded nice, she'd never had cake that wasn't, but whenever she was in a strange world she always felt a desire to try something new.

"Tea and the, er... Eccles Cake then," she replied brightly, after a moment's thought.

The lady didn't seem to need her pen and paper, the order was obviously easy enough to remember.

Sitting quietly and relaxing in nice warm surroundings was always the best place to contemplate the future, and the small tea room on a main street had offered a handy retreat. If truth be known this wasn't an ideal place, it was still a strange world full of strange things and people, but it was likely there were no immediate threats here. The lady with the pen behind her ear seemed pretty chilled, and didn't look like much of a street fighter, although appearances could easily be deceptive. She'd been caught out many moons ago by that strange creature with the wrinkled face and the blue hair and the walking stick... but no, this seemed a fairly safe place to sit and relax and take stock of the situation. At least here no-one was trying to kill her, and that was one of the pressing subjects that needed her attention.

The dream. Now that she had a chance to think it through a bit more it was beginning to make sense.

It wasn't her that had been moving around in that dream. She'd been in the mind of someone, or something, else, which could only be the bow-and-arrow creature. What she'd been seeing and feeling was what it was seeing and feeling. That was why she hadn't had any control over what was happening. She'd been a passenger. She was watching the girl getting rescued, and she'd seen details in the dream that she hadn't seen from where she was stood, so it wasn't just something her brain had made up. She'd been looking at it from a different viewpoint. It had been rather interesting and very worrying. The rather interesting thing was that she hadn't seen herself through its eyes, and it had been looking right at the place where she had been standing. That meant the hunter man, which she was now convinced it was, couldn't see her, even though she hadn't been trying especially hard to hide. So, it couldn't see auras like she could, and that was good. The very worrying thing was, well, there were actually several very worrying things. For a start it had been right there just across from where she was stood, and she hadn't been aware of it, which meant it could have shot her and she wouldn't have known what had hit her. More worrying was that it had followed her from the world where the car crash occurred, to the world where the settlers rescued the girl. Or more likely, she had taken it with them, along with the boulders, and it had gone off after the family in the direction of the settlement.

That was all she remembered about the dream, apart from the feeling of excitement that it had felt when it realised there was something to hunt. They were probably easy prey though, lumbering along, carrying an injured girl and therefore not able to run and fight very well, but still, the thrill of the chase was all that had mattered to it.

"Here you are dear," said a voice.

The lady with the pen behind her ear unloaded a cup and saucer from her tray onto the table, followed by a pot of tea, and a little jug of milk. "...and your cake," she continued, producing a small plate containing an object that looked like the circle of wood that was left in a hole saw after you'd finished making the cut-out for a drainpipe.

Jennifer had opened her mouth and was just about to say "No... I ordered cake!" when she realised that the pen-behind-the-ear lady had gone, and was now away in the back of the shop somewhere, rattling something.

Putting the saucer to one side, she poured herself a cup of tea. Saucers were, well, too dainty. A step too far. There was plenty of tea in the pot for a mug, so quite why it was necessary to keep refilling a little cup was a mystery to her. A spot of milk made it perfect which, on reflection was better than her life at the moment. She often looked back on her adult life with a sense of regret, but that was her own fault of course. Although Aylas couldn't change their form to any significant extent from day to day, it was possible to travel to another time where you were younger, provided of course that you weren't already there. That was impossible, and a ridiculous idea anyway. She had been told that, if you conjured up the image of where and when you wanted to be, and also convinced yourself that you were the age you wanted to be, it could be done. Nobody recommended it, but when you were young and adventurous and up for new challenges you got dragged along with an idea, and sometimes tried things that you subsequently regretted. After having a big argument one day, someone close to her had suggested they went back to being children again, and she'd agreed. She had thought it might be a way to solve a problem that was destroying her life at the time, and it had seemed like a solution. It had taken some doing. It hadn't been easy to totally convince herself that she was back at home and six years old, but it had worked. She winced at the thought, and gritted her teeth. Never again that was for sure. Nobody else she knew had tried it. Perhaps that was because they could imagine what the body had to go through to fit itself into something that was about half its previous size, and then re-adjust to making that body work.

There had been advantages, of course. On the one hand it was useful because she could do things almost unnoticed. Nobody was too concerned about what a little girl did, she was almost invisible in plain sight. But on the other hand, it hadn't helped her to get any more boyfriends.

Could she have simply done the reverse and gone back to being an adult again? Probably, but that sounded as if it might have been even more painful. Trying to become larger when there isn't enough of you to make something that big would surely be even worse. It sounded like it ought to involve having your arms and legs torn out of their sockets. No – she would just grow up again, that was the best plan. It wasn't every day that you could live your life over, armed with the knowledge that you could only have gained by having grown up once before. That had been a few years ago, and she'd almost forgotten what it was like to be an adult, but being with the hunter? Yes! That had felt exciting. He was a character. It had felt good to view the world through the eyes of something big again. To be able to move so effortlessly, without having to drag little legs along underneath you, and just that feeling, of being so alive and carefree and so strong. Not being responsible for anything. That had been good, but also somehow scary. She wanted more of it, but didn't know why.

She considered her plate with some suspicion before picking up the thing that had been proffered as 'cake'.

It looked like a piece of chipboard with dead flies in it.

She examined it more closely. No, it was what they called 'flaky pastry'. Not spongy like the cake she usually ate. She gave it an experimental sniff and knew what it was almost at once. Flaky pastry with dried fruit in it. Currants by the look of them.

It was probably called cake because it went hard when it went stale. That was the definition of 'cake' in most worlds, as she understood it. Cake went hard, biscuits went soft, that's how you decided whether to call something a cake or a biscuit. It tasted nice. She turned the words over in her mouth and made a mental note. So, *Eccles Cake* then. A treat to remember.

She topped up her cup with more tea, and turned her thoughts to something else that had been troubling her ever since she'd fallen asleep in the hollow the previous night.

Here she was. Home from an adventure, looking forward to peace and quiet but off on another instead. The invitation from someone she hadn't seen in years. All the stuff with the secret symbols. The Council and the bow-and-arrow man. Alkira's cave. Coming here. Finding the hunter so quickly. Something had been niggling at her for a while now, but she couldn't put her finger on it. Something wasn't right. Something didn't make sense, and that was the problem. It had all happened so quickly, and it all fitted together too well.

In a rack on the wall behind her were some leaflets showing attractions and places to visit in the area. She picked out a few and looked at the pictures. It seemed to be a popular place. She couldn't read the writing but there were pictures of lots of things to do and see.

The ability to speak and understand a lot of languages came with the job, but the writing in most worlds was very strange. She was used to dealing with symbols that meant unique things, what many civilisations would call 'nouns'. She had no use for descriptive words like 'big' and 'small' – she just drew a bigger symbol or a smaller one. There was no need to draw anything about time either. Nothing she drew needed to have any concept of time in it, so there were no symbols for abstract things like yesterday, today and tomorrow, and no concept of things concerning past or future events like 'has been', or 'will be'. Symbols were either there or they weren't. Things either existed or they didn't. There was only one picture of a world.

Languages involving writing instead of drawing were very difficult. She could never get the hang of them. One particular leaflet, a green one, had lots of pictures of trees and forests on it, but also the writing looked as if it contained many different words. She didn't know what any of them meant, but she could tell that a lot of them weren't repeated, so it would probably be a reasonably good representation of how they wrote things here.

She folded that one up and put it in her pocket. If she came out of this mess alive and this world was still here, she was going to find a good use for it.

After finishing up her cake and emptying the teacup, she left the tea room when the pen-behind-the-ear lady was rattling about again in the back of the shop, made her way quickly up the street, and turned right at the next corner.

This really was a nice day. She'd almost dried out now, still a bit damp around the waist, and her hair was going to go curly if she didn't find a way to dry it properly with a brush, but hey, worse things could happen. There was nothing wrong with curly hair.

It was a shame about running away without paying, she thought, but that was life in a strange world. She didn't have any money and no sensible way to get any without taking it from someone else, which wouldn't help her conscience. The lady in the shop had been very nice. She would find a way to make it up to her. In some worlds the people somehow knew these things were done by 'karma', but they only pretended to understand it.

The shop owner would probably be cursing, and thinking that karma would make sure the girl would get what she deserved for being such a little rat. However, when something good happened unexpectedly to the shop lady at some point in the future, you could bet she wouldn't be thinking "Oh, this is a reward from that little girl who didn't pay". Karma really did work in mysterious ways.

Her situation was different now. There was no point in going back to the road and the ledge and the river. The hunter was gone, he was in the world with the girl and the settlements. She needed to make sure the girl was kept safe because that world clearly had some plans for her, she was somehow important, and she also needed to find out more about the hunter. There was also something troubling about the events of the last couple of days at home too, which was niggling at her.

She found a comfortable place to sit in the sunshine and snooze for the remainder of the day in a nearby park. Then, when the sun had climbed overhead, and the heat of the day began to turn to late afternoon, she made her way out along what looked like the main street, in search of a place away from the lights of the town. There were people around, but no-one paid her any attention.

There was no doubt about it, being alone was difficult. Nobody cared, and you had to look after yourself. You could fight, try to play the hero and suffer for it, but sometimes you had to do what was best for you.

That was why she was going back to the worlds she knew best. Not because she was giving up, but because it had turned out to be more difficult than she had imagined. It needed a better plan, and rethinking it was the sensible thing to do. A lot of branches had spread out across many different worlds, changing them all in unpredictable ways. There were fundamental things she didn't feel comfortable with, but more importantly, she also had a sense there were more things she needed to understand, and doing that would present her with an easier way to approach the problem.

Further along the street was a large clump of trees with pink blossoms. When she got nearer, she could see it was a church, an ornate stone building with a tall spire and a little black iron fence along the front. It seemed to be a gathering place. The blossom was falling and drifting in the gentle warm breeze, carpeting the street in a blanket of pink. Bells were clanging softly in the tower. She recognised the style of the building. People built them all over the place, in almost every world, to glorify their creator. Personally, she'd never liked the idea, and she wouldn't be particularly grateful to have one built in her honour, but they looked nice.

A girl was standing by the railings holding a small cap in front of her with both hands.

"Hey! Any change?" she called to Jennifer as she walked past.

Jennifer turned and took a step towards her.

The girl was about her size and looked to be about the same age. The cap contained a few coins.

"What for?" she asked, putting her head slightly to one side in a quizzical pose.

The girl didn't think for long. There were probably a lot of things she could have said. She made something up.

"For a little girl with no home?"

"Good try," thought Jennifer. "I... don't have any money?" she replied, attempting to sound sad.

The girl looked at her with a little appealing face, and then seemed to recognise a kindred spirit.

"Oh well," she said softly, "it was worth a try."

"It certainly was," replied Jennifer. She knew what a professional beggar was, of course, every world had those as well. They lurked almost everywhere that people congregated, and by a church where people were gathering was the perfect place to stand. She'd never thought much about beggars, but she had suddenly realised that here was someone who made their entire living by asking everyone to help them. It raised some interesting questions.

"I liked that little touch," said the girl.

"What?" asked Jennifer.

"The head on one side," she replied, copying it. "It's cute. I must remember that."

"Tell me, do you make much?"

The girl seemed somewhat affronted by this unexpected turn of events.

"Er... sometimes. If you can catch the right people and make up the right responses."

"You don't seem to have a lot of money in there right now," replied Jennifer, looking into the cap.

"No," replied the girl. "You don't keep everything in your cap. Someone would knock it out of your hand and steal it. You put most of it in your pocket, and just keep a bit of change out so that people have more sympathy because it makes you look poor."

Jennifer thought that had merit. When she was cornered, she did that to people all the time. It was fine doing a great job, creating and maintaining and fixing worlds, but nobody cared, and nobody ever gave you anything. You were just a nothing, and nobody even knew who you were.

The girl had wandered away. "Any change lady?" she called to another passer-by, a well-endowed woman who looked like she wasn't short of money. "For a little girl who's lost her parents!"

The lady looked at her with a sad face, and seemed to take pity on her. Something was put into the cap.

"Thank you!" cried the girl, and scuttled back towards Jennifer.

"Now we take that out," she said brightly, pulling the paper note from the cap and stuffing it in her pocket. "Otherwise, people think you're doing well and don't need their help."

"So, how do you get people to give you money then?" asked Jennifer.

"It's easy. Just ask them for it," she replied, brightly, with a smile.

"And they just give it to you, do they?" said Jennifer, unconvinced.

"Sometimes they have questions. But you just look at them, weigh them up, try to work out who they are and how they think, and then tell them what they want to hear," she said.

Jennifer thought that was interesting. To make people do what you want just ask them, and tell them what they want to hear.

It was true though. Nobody on the street knew whether the girl had a home or not, and nobody knew whether she had any parents or not, but if you asked them for help and told them a good story, they'd give you something, because it made them feel better about themselves. That was the trick, play to their conscience. She'd never got the hang of that bit.

"I've nearly collected enough now for today," said the girl. "And then I can go home," she added.

"Oh well, sorry. I'm a stranger here and I really don't have any money at all, but thank you for your time," she added. "Hope you have a good day!"

With that she turned, and continued along the road away from the bustle of the town.

"I will!" called the girl.

Jennifer looked back and waved. The girl smiled.

After a while Jennifer came to a bus shelter on a quiet stretch of the street, which seemed like a good place to sit and think until it got dark.

Perhaps it was true. If you played the game right, people would give you things and do things for you just because you asked them. You didn't have to actually do anything yourself. Just ask in the right way and they would do it for you because it made them feel happier about themselves. It made them feel they'd done the right thing, and that would be the only reward they needed.

After an hour or so, the sky behind the patches of grey cloud started to turn orange, and the birds began to settle into their snug little places for the night.

It was time for her to go too, but not to bed.

There was work to be done.

Things were not as they seemed to be. Some things had been too good to be true, but some things had also been too bad to be true.

In the quietness, she began to recall some memories... of a cave, and a different deep orange sunset, and the yellow sands of a rolling desert with a warm wind that blew wisps of sand off the tops of the dunes... and a small stick propped against the wall, the marker which she'd left to fix the time accurately in an otherwise timeless world. Imagery formed in her mind of the place she wanted to be. She could see it, smell it, touch it, and when she opened her eyes, she would be there.

At this time of night there were no passers-by, so nobody saw her shadowy shape fade away gently into the darkness, until no trace remained to indicate she had ever existed.

11 - It Starts

In the beginning there was nothing.

Only The Word.

And The Word looked around and said: "Oooo! It's dark, isn't it!".

So, The Word created light.

But that wasn't much help because there was nothing to see, except a lot of space.

So, The Word created some things for the light to shine off.

They looked nice.

"That's better," it thought.

So, it created some more things, and they looked nice as well.

It was fun.

After working on it for a week, The Word was fed up. Space seemed to be very big, and growing faster than it could make things to fill it up.

So, The Word made things that could make things, and it called them 'life'.

"That will solve my problems," it thought.

Then it got itself a mug of tea, and a big piece of cake, and sat back to watch.

Those words, or some variation of them, appear on the walls of caves and in the written legends of most civilisations.

In this modern age, hardly anyone seriously believes them because they are too full of inconsistencies, but in various isolated parts of the universe, some collections of life do take them seriously, and in the absence of any further communication from said 'Word', have formed their own opinions of subsequent likely events.

Some believe that The Word is still drinking tea and eating cake, and watching, perhaps applauding their attempts to create new things for the light to shine off, and is tweaking everything now and again as it sees fit.

Others take a more pragmatic view and believe that The Word has probably drunk a lot of tea and eaten a lot of cake, and has fallen asleep a long time ago, which is why their worlds are in such a mess. They eagerly await the time they call 'The Great Awakening' when The Word will stir from its slumbers and look upon their work with pride, and perhaps offer them some tea and cake.

Still others, however, await this moment somewhat apprehensively, believing that, when The Word does finally awaken after drinking lots of tea and sleeping for eons, it will have more pressing uses for their work than to look upon it. These civilisations have, for some reason, become prolific boat builders.

Nowadays, many people who feel a pressing need to know the answer to something that would be of no use to them even if they knew it, think this might be how the first Ayla came to be drawn. This, of course, is all conjecture because no-one was there to see it happen.

Cut into the side of a sandstone mountain in a world where nobody builds any boats, is a big cave with smudges on the wall. A pair of big dark eyes is examining them in great detail and, at this point in time, their owner is giving considerable thought to the subject of how they came to exist.

"Mmmm..." it says to itself, thoughtfully.

Lines are being drawn from smudge to smudge, notes are being scribbled on empty patches of wall. Symbols are passing in front of its eyes. It's looking. Working. Analysing. Thinking. Grubby fingers are leaving more marks on the already dirty face of a little girl, who spends a lot of her time trying to keep curls of black hair behind her ears and away from her face.

The sun passes relentlessly across the opening of the cave, changing the hues of the desert and dunes from a searing white inferno to endless folds of soft reds and oranges. The evening wind picks up, and a little stick topples into the sand which is accumulating at the bottom of the wall.

Lists are being created. Entries are being made. Conclusions are being drawn.

Eventually the task is over, and the girl steps away from the wall. She makes one final and futile attempt at tucking her black curly hair behind her ears, before allowing herself a big breath, followed by an equally big sigh. It has taken her all night, and most of the following day, but the effort has been worthwhile.

It was just as she had thought.

What she had been led to believe was wrong, but it would have been easy to miss. It was only because she'd studied it in great detail that she knew the truth, or some of it anyway.

She sat down on the dusty floor near the mouth of the cave for the first time since she had arrived, and looked out across the world. She now knew that the information she'd been given was wrong, and that was very worrying.

The next step would be to go back to her home in the tunnels, find Alkira, who should be looking after it, and see what she had to say for herself. Somebody wasn't telling the truth.

To complicate things, the bow-and-arrow man was loose in the other world, a danger to the girl and the settlers, and probably still doing whatever it was that he did that destroyed worlds. There were too many things that needed tending to. She ought to be there as well, but it would all have to wait until tomorrow. Sleep was calling, and she needed time to let the new information sink in, and time to think about exactly what she would do when she got home, and how she would deal with whatever she found there.

The ground was warm but very gritty and not a good place to sleep, so she went away into the back of the cave in search of a bed.

***

The next day was another puzzle. It felt like mid-morning when she woke and dusted herself off. Something else she had found last night, or in fact *not* found last night, had raised even more questions, and she had been relieved to be going home, back to her comfy little existence in the tunnels. What she saw when she got there was very revealing.

The mugs had tea stains in the bottom of them, the kettle was cold, and the stove had gone out. Nothing in the little room had moved.

The supply of candles had not been replenished, and everything was just the way she had left it several days ago when she'd first taken Alkira's hand.

Alkira was supposed to be looking after her worlds, but she wasn't here, and it looked like she had never been here. If she'd been doing anything here, she hadn't been drinking, eating or sleeping, and if she'd been working in the tunnels, it would have been mostly in the dark, which wasn't likely.

That put an end to the first part of the idea she'd formulated, which was to not let on about the discoveries of last night, and to sit down with Alkira to ask some more questions about how the worlds in the cave had got destroyed.

Those things would have to go on hold for the moment. Plan 'A' had failed but that didn't matter. People who set out to succeed didn't just have one plan. There was something she needed to find now, something from the past which might shed a light on the future. She strode off through the dark corridors towards the very back of the tunnel complex.

There was no danger of walking into anything or losing her way. Even in the dark she knew exactly where everything was.

As she progressed deeper into the maze of tunnels, the smells began to change. The air became more musty, and somehow old, as if it hadn't been breathed for years. After five more minutes of brisk walking, she stopped and felt for a shelf. Yes! There was still a candle on it, and a lighter. It felt like one of the very old, tapered candles she used to burn years ago. It was as she had suspected, no-one had been in this part of the complex for a very long time.

Striking up the flame revealed memories of the past.

The room in front of her was full of toys and books and things she'd kept from her first childhood. A bit of dust, but not much considering no-one had disturbed anything for years.

She pulled items out of the piles carefully, and stacked them up near the entrance.

Hah! Teddy bears. Jigsaw puzzles. A skipping rope – she'd never got the hang of that. One roller skate. A stuffed elephant – a toy, not a real one - and a xylophone with one of the coloured chime bars missing.

...and somewhere at the back there should be a trunk.

She found it under a bundle of old clothes. Some of the bigger ones would probably fit her now, she thought.

Working through all her old stuff was a strange experience, but everybody kept things. Just because she was an Ayla didn't mean she had to throw her childhood away.

And here it was, an old wooden trunk with a hinged lid, and a leather strap around it to keep it shut. She knew what would be in it.

Magic.

That's what she would find.

Answers, and hopefully the solution to the last little problem that had been niggling at her ever since she took the unexpected trip in the mind of the bow-and-arrow creature.

The strap came undone easily.

You could be forgiven for expecting the lid to creak open ominously, revealing some kind of mystical glowing entity that had the power to change the world, or something like that.

What it revealed however was an oracle with the power to answer all her questions.

A load of old books.

Thick hardback books, some of them leather bound, with dented corners and scuffs on the covers. All the ones from the bookshelf in the house where she had grown up it seemed, and hopefully the ones from the locked cabinet with the glass doors as well.

That was the prize. Those were the special books. One in particular. If it wasn't here she would be very worried, and she'd have to rethink her assumptions, yet again.

Kneeling on the ground, she began to pick them out and stack them up in heaps on the floor. Most of them were recognisable as the ones from the shelves, because they had dusty tops to them and sun-bleached spines. She opened one at random and turned a few pages. The symbols seemed to be about something she recognised as *space travel*. That would have belonged to her father. He'd always been interested in visiting other worlds, but her parents were only human. She had fond memories of her father, and it would be worth a read one day, but it wasn't what she was looking for right now.

Next to it, as if they had perhaps been originally stacked side by side, were two pocket notebooks with purple covers which she could not recall ever having seen before. They were blank, apart from inscriptions on the inside cover, in her father's handwriting. After a moment's thought, she stuffed them both carefully in her pocket.

About two thirds of the way through the layers, the books she was pulling out began to look newer, tidier. Yes! These were the ones from the cabinet, and hopefully the one she wanted was amongst them. It was *the* book, the definitive book, well, a copy of it. Probably a first edition, not that very many copies would have been made anyway. From what she could remember it may well have been handwritten, she couldn't be sure.

Little motes of dust sparkled in the light from the candle as the piles on the floor grew bigger. Not this one. Not this one. It was a thin book, smaller format than most of the others, almost as if it had been designed to be a field guide.

And suddenly there it was, standing on its end at the back of the trunk! A slimmer hardback book with a red leather cover and the title stamped in faded gold leaf. She lifted it out reverently and held it closer to the candle. The symbols didn't translate directly to the language she'd been used to speaking these last few years, but they went straight into her brain, and she knew exactly what most of them meant. She spoke them to herself, almost in a whisper. This was what she had been looking for:

The Creator's Guide to Tertiary Creatures

The light from the tiny flame flickered across the pages as she sat cross-legged on the floor holding the book in her lap. She could feel warmth on her leg, but she wasn't sure whether it was from the candle, or the book.

The candle seemed to be lasting long enough. That was good. If you went out of the room and turned left twice, about two minutes' walk, there should be at least two more on the shelf just near the tunnel that held some of her older works, but two minutes was too long to stop reading the book for.

It was strange going back to reading stories written in symbols, instead of drawing them to create works of art. It was difficult, but exciting. She'd not read storybooks for years, and this was a type of storybook. The symbols didn't all make sense as far as telling a narrative was concerned, they were designed to represent physical 'things', not actions, so getting her mind around their implications was a challenge.

The other problem was that the writing couldn't contain the symbols it was talking about. You wouldn't write the symbols for the actual creatures in the book. It wouldn't matter if there was nothing to gather around them, but if you drew the symbols in a book, and they somehow became exposed to the essences of life, there would be trouble.

For that reason, those symbols were drawn naïvely and disjointed, so they looked enough like the proper symbols for the reader to know what they were, but not enough to behave like them. That of course assumed the reader knew what the proper symbols looked like in the first place.

It was fascinating.

It showed how to draw them, told you what prerequisites they needed to become activated, what creatures they created, and what each creature did.

Some of the descriptions also had a couple of rows at the end of the page which looked as if they listed the pros and cons, or the advantages and dangers. These were written as sequences of symbols drawn in green or red, presumably green for good and red for bad. You'd hope so anyway, or maybe it would be the other way round just to fool people who didn't know what they were doing and shouldn't have been reading it anyway.

There were far more of the third-level symbols than she had remembered Alkira telling her about, but some were very obscure, and even the book held little information about them.

She recognised the section about Aylas. Its symbol was split up into three sequences of strokes that were clearly meant to be drawn on top of each other, but its meaning was obvious.

There was a section about the creature represented by the letter 'K', containing some revelations, including what looked like a note indicating that, as she expected, only one of them should be drawn. The symbol for 'K' followed by the mark for '1' in green, the symbol for 'K' followed by the symbol for 'many', in red, and also three symbols for 'K' in red, presumably in case the reader didn't recognise the symbol for many.

That would also enable the reader to deduce the symbol for 'many' if they hadn't known it. That was how you had to write a book if it was supposed to be a book about how to read.

Every Ayla had dealings with 'K', it was hard to imagine how anyone could come to terms with creating and destroying people and their worlds without requiring the services of 'K'. Everyone knew how to summon her, but it was likely that hardly any of them knew where she came from.

It was a book that she'd never been allowed to look at in any depth when she was a child, and she found it fascinating.

When she turned a page and saw the symbol for a bow-and-arrow creature, she took a sharp intake of breath. Yes! It was here. Not as she had seen it drawn of course, but as several disjointed strokes. The bow was drawn as a curve, with the string not connected to it, and the arrow wasn't drawn across it, but separately, with the 'v' marks that represented the tip and the flight not joined to the ends.

There wasn't much about it on the page, but from what she could see, it first needed a world with life. Yes, and complex life. Almost all of them did, nothing new there.

There were seemingly no advantages to creating one, she noted as she ran her finger over the symbols, as if feeling them somehow helped to understand them. Inexplicably, it did. Disadvantages, er… destruction of your world – ooh – that was nasty, but not surprising. It told of a couple of things to do and not to do, but they were nothing she didn't already know, just stuff that mostly applied to all tertiary creatures.

When she scanned the symbols on the last few lines, her expression slowly froze into a mask of total disbelief. After a long moment she read on, but she didn't need to. She now understood exactly what the implications were, and her world was never going to be the same.

***

And now it was very late. The candle flame had long ago sputtered and died. The book had been replaced in the trunk, along with all the others, and the remnants of childhood re-stacked around it. All in the dark. She didn't need light to know where they all went. She couldn't put the dust back, but it didn't matter. It was a good bet that no-one else knew about this room, but even if they found it, they wouldn't know the book existed.

The secret was safe.

Jennifer wandered back through the tunnels in darkness to her room above the valley. It had only taken her a few minutes to get back, but it had seemed like an eternity.

She sat and stared at the woodgrain on her tabletop while the little stove heated up. It took ages. That was what happened when you let it go out and get completely cold, she thought.

There were several truths about learning. She'd always known that. On the one hand you knew what you knew. It was obvious, although sometimes you did forget that you knew something.

You also knew there were things you didn't know about. That was good too, because you could go and find out about them.

The danger lay in the list of things that you didn't know you didn't know. There was nothing you could do about that, except to keep looking and learning, and in that process you'd discover things that you never suspected.

The water in the kettle boiled and she sat back down at the table with a mug of tea.

The bow-and-arrow man. The destroyer of worlds. That was what people thought, and that was what the book had said the symbol created. A dangerous creature, and no information as to how to destroy it once it had been brought into existence.

However, the book had told her *why* you would draw it and what its purpose was, and she now knew what she had to do.

You couldn't eliminate it, but you could stop it being destructive, and the way to do that was to satisfy its desires. She would have to give it what it wanted, and if everything she'd seen over the last few days stacked up the way she thought, she had a pretty good idea what that would be. The creature had seemed to connect with her when she had fallen asleep in the forest. It had seemed to like being linked with her mind, but she wasn't ready to fall prey to a hunter. Jennifer knew it wasn't going to be easy. Most times when you fought a battle you faced some foe, or enemy. No matter how powerful they were, you could find a way to destroy them, somehow. To win this battle she would have to face reality. To destroy that, sacrifices would have to be made.

She reached out to the message frame on the wall above the table, and her fingers moved slowly across the smooth grey concrete surface. What she was looking for would be tucked in the bottom corner somewhere. Yes, there it was! She leaned across and gently blew the covering of dust out of the way. Tiny specks floated lazily in the moonbeams which came through the gaps in the vines as the cartouche began to appear out of the dust. A little outline, in which were written the letters 'JM'. She hadn't seen it for years, but she had always known it was there. Despite having cleaned out all the symbols she never used, that one had remained. She had never imagined how the day might come when she would actually want to use it, but it was something that she could never bring herself to erase.

Well, there really wasn't any other choice.

That day was today.

She reached out very slowly and caressed it gently. The thoughts of what it might do didn't make her flinch in the way she had imagined it might. Perhaps things wouldn't be as bad as she thought. After a moment she took a breath and came to a conclusion. She really had to do this.

Maybe it wouldn't be possible after all this time, maybe it wouldn't work, but she had to try.

She touched it more firmly with two fingers.

Nothing happened.

That wasn't good. Perhaps, she thought, it no longer works, and that was an extremely uncomfortable feeling because it would mean there was nothing on the other end of it anymore.

After a moment, the outline of the letters began to flicker faintly with an orange glow and then, slower than a heartbeat, the symbol began to flash.

She took her fingers away, and watched the symbol for a moment or two.

A new plan was forming but it needed thought, and time to flesh out the details. A sneaky feeling told her that she wasn't going to get it.

It was set in motion now. What would happen would happen.

Perhaps she would be able to make it work, and perhaps she wouldn't, but the courage was to at least try. That was what made you brave. Not doing something that others were afraid to do, but doing something that *you* were afraid to do.

She would have to see what morning would bring, but not before a good wash, and some time spent getting her hair straight again.

12 - The Long Goodbye

Jennifer awoke, but it wasn't morning. There was a figure standing in the shadows at the end of the room. It didn't move, and she had the feeling that it was watching her. She reached up to the shelf and lit the candle. The shape was still there. She got out of bed and walked slowly towards it. As she got nearer, she could see that it was a girl. The candle was still on the shelf, but the flame gave enough light to see by. The figure was the same height and build as she was, with exactly the same style of long dark hair, standing motionless with her arms loosely by her side. As her eyes began to adjust to the dim light, she could see the girl's face better. It was almost like looking into a mirror.

For a moment she was taken aback. It had worked! It was what she had asked for, but it had happened so quickly. She'd thought it would have taken more time, or perhaps not worked at all, but here she was, looking at what appeared to be an exact copy of herself.

Their eyes met, a tingle ran down her spine, and suddenly the memories came flooding back. The endless summer days spent riding their bikes across the fields, picking daisies, laughing and rolling down the little hills. Laying on the riverbank in the warm sunshine with grubby hands and faces, watching the birds and the clouds, and being late home for tea.

And then the world had slowly gone wrong. They'd grown up.

There had been better things to do than ride bicycles and explore caves, fly kites and have adventures. They'd become tired of each other's company.

Real life had got in the way, and then there were boys.

They'd fought, argued, learned to hate each other over trivialities. Had different dreams.

Then one day it had seemed like going back to being six years old would solve both their problems.

It hadn't, because you could get your childhood body back, but not the innocence that came with it. Once you'd learned something you were never the same again. It wasn't possible to unlearn it, and it wasn't possible to ever forget.

They'd fought even more after that. Gone their separate ways and lived under different skies in different worlds. Vowed never to speak to each other again. It hadn't seemed possible that the two of them would ever stand together again on the same piece of earth. And now, here she was, after all this time.

It was hardly believable, but she'd accepted the invitation, which was a start, and so far, neither of them had tried to rip the other's eyes out.

Finally, it was the girl in the shadows who broke the uneasy silence.

"Hello Sis," she said.

***

The sight of the two figures sat facing each other across the table looked like some kind of 'through the looking glass' sculpture.

Jennifer had produced another mug from somewhere in the storage space under the floor. It was identical to the one she had been using, so you couldn't even tell the sisters apart by what mug they were holding.

"...I don't care, there was no need to burn all my clothes!"
"And the boy I liked?"
Jennifer shook her head sadly, as if considering the value of regretting something, and deciding it served no purpose.

"It's not my fault if he couldn't tell us apart..." she said, her voice trailing off at the end as if there should be more to say, but there wasn't.

"I've never forgotten y'know."

"No. I don't suppose you have."

"And here you are living in a pipe, and you really think *my* lifestyle is crap!"

"I never said it was…"

"Yeah, you did! You always said that cities were horrible."

"That's not true – I just think that the combination of things you believe in doesn't add up…"

"...to a healthy existence. Yeah, I know, but at least I have some artistic *style*…"

"Oh – I see. All the trendy rubbish in your life counts as *style* then…"

They were still bickering when the shafts of early morning sunlight started to break through the vines and make pretty patterns on the table.

Her sister, Jackie, blinked as one of them caught her in the eye.

"Anyway," she said sadly. "Here we are."

There was a long, quiet, uneasy moment where neither sister wanted to make eye contact.

Jennifer looked up from her mug, and Jackie looked down at hers. Neither of them really knew *where* they should look. The mugs weren't interesting anymore, and the woodgrain on the table had long ago surrendered to all forms of analysis.

"So, what do we do?" asked Jennifer quietly.

They both knew that if there was any hope of being friends again, they would have to start a clean sheet. After all this time you would have thought it would be easy. It wasn't. Neither of them wanted to surrender, and neither of them wanted to be the first to give in. Jennifer knew it would never be possible to forget what had happened between them, it would never be possible to bury it, and never be possible to ignore it.

If you wanted to make any progress, all you could do was just accept what had happened in the past and move on.

It was as simple as that.

No matter what the world had thrown at them, they were sisters.

There had to be a future. Something for both of them. If they wanted it.

Jennifer moved her hand, and that was all it took. Jackie leaned towards her with her arms outstretched. They wrapped themselves around each other, put their heads on each other's shoulders, and began to cry.

***

Now the little stove was working overtime. They had just returned from Jennifer showing Jackie some of her new drawings, which meant ones a little deeper in the tunnel complex that had been created in the last five or six years, so yet more tea was being made.

It wasn't the sort of creative art that Jackie appreciated, she was more of a street artist kind of creator. Drawing things by the book wasn't her scene.

Lovely worlds that were tuned incrementally by altering the subtle tinges of the colours of life over a long period of time didn't really float her boat.

That was just one of the differences that had fuelled their disagreements long ago. Jackie was never able to maintain a degree of enthusiasm and dedication for anything. She got fed up easily and didn't have any patience with life, not even her own. Most of her drawings were half-baked worlds, abandoned, never to be completed. Strange experimental existences with lots of rock and dust and wind, but no water, were extended until they filled a whole wall.

The templates for life she drew in those barely inhabitable worlds were not much better. Creatures with long necks, and big grey things with enormous noses that looked like hosepipes. It was cruel, that's what it was!

Jennifer liked things to *evolve* over long periods. She felt it produced better quality life-forms than meddling with them all the time. Let life design itself, that was best, and only tinker with it if it looked like it was messing itself up.

Her sister needed reminding how a proper well-designed natural world worked. At some point, she would take Jackie out to experience the countryside again. It had to be done. Even though she was sure her sister wouldn't like it, Jennifer needed the downtime with Jackie to chill and talk if her plan was to work.

There were two ways to get down to the forest in the valley.

The hard way was to go to the top of the hill by climbing up the ladder in the main ventilation pipe and opening the metal grate. Then you could take the small rocky path that snaked down the gentler slope at the back of the hill past the fire pit, and walk all the way along the stream to get round to the valley, which took about an hour.

The easier and quicker way was to go to the end of pipe T45, and slide down the concrete water channel with your bum stuck in a wok.

When you had the body of a six-year-old and you were trying to regain your childhood, the prospect of riding a helter skelter from the top of the world to the bottom was an exciting one. It had sounded like a fantastic game.

Jennifer had tried it once. The principle was sound, but not the implementation. There hadn't been any skin left on her knuckles by the time she'd got halfway down because there was nothing to keep the wok in the middle of the channel. Apart from that, a child sitting in a metal saucer isn't very stable and it had tipped over and spilled her out, which had saved her knuckles from further destruction, but she'd fallen through the treetops at the bottom with grazes all over her arms and legs, a lump smashed out of the side of her head, a dislocated shoulder, and two broken fingers. That was before she'd hit the ground. Most of the injuries had sorted themselves out over time, but putting the shoulder back had been extremely painful, and limping up the hill to get home had taken her all day.

Today, Jennifer and Jackie were... walking as far as the fire pit!

And talking. And planning. Almost dancing along the narrow path in the sunshine with a spring in their step and recalling past adventures.

"...and do you remember that world full of soldiers?"

"Oh, yeah!" replied Jackie. "They were indestructible, weren't they."

"Well, no," replied Jennifer cheekily, "because we destroyed them!"

"Yeah, but they were *supposed* to be indestructible. They *thought* they were indestructible. They had those bulletproof jacket things... made of Kevin or something..."

"Kevlar" interrupted Jennifer.

"Yeah, Kevlar. That was it!"

"Most of their body was covered up, and they had helmets on too."

"Made 'em hard to kill."

"There were bits you could shoot at like arms and legs, but that didn't really kill them," said Jennifer.

"No, it just made 'em more angry, and there were hundreds of 'em, almost everywhere you turned."

"But we did find a way didn't we! Do you remember?"

"Oh yeah, I remember!" grinned Jackie. "There were bits we could shoot them through that they couldn't cover up very well. Made a mess, but it killed 'em."

The sisters turned towards each other, and raised their hands for a high-five.

"Eyeballs!" they shouted in unison.

"Yeah! The good old days," said Jackie, playfully.

"We did have some fun together," agreed her sister.

As they rounded the curve of the hillside, Jennifer motioned to the left. The fire pit was set back just off the path, with a view across the canopy of mixed woodland treetops in the valley, which seemed to go on forever, lush and damp, with little clouds of condensation sitting above them here and there. She had used the area as a temporary place to live while she was fitting out her little room, before she had a wood-burning stove and proper furniture. There were two smooth, flat boulders that could be used as seats, although she almost never had anyone to sit with. Besides being useful for cooking, the fire kept away most predators, you could dry your clothes by it, and curl up beside it at night to keep warm. It had served her well. As far as she was concerned, every civilised person needed a fire pit. In recent years the room overlooking the valley had become her only home because it was convenient to live nearer to her work, and the room was definitely more comfortable. She almost never used the fire pit anymore. Perhaps she was going soft in her old age, she thought.

When they were finally settled there, Jennifer felt it would be a good opportunity to mention the visit she had made to the twisted land to look for the bow-and-arrow creature.

Her sister appeared surprised at that revelation.

"Oh! I thought you might have heard about it, but I never expected you'd go after it," she squeaked.

"Mmmm," replied Jennifer, twiddling her fingers thoughtfully. "The Council asked me to go and check it out."

"Really! Rumour has it that The Council sent people to kill it, but they never came back."

"Yes, that's what I heard too. You might be surprised to learn that I did track it down," winced Jennifer, trying to shake off the memory of the huge metal monster with yellow eyes. "I don't know exactly what it is, or what it's doing, but I have found out... some things..." she added, thoughtfully, not wanting to give away too much.

Jackie remained silent, as if she could think of nothing to add to the conversation.

"The Council seemed to think that I could maybe do something about it... because I'm just a little girl," continued Jennifer. "But it looks like it's going to be a bigger job than I had originally thought. I don't think I'll be able to do it on my own."

"So, are you suggesting we do it together?" asked Jackie, after a moment's contemplation.

This was exactly what Jennifer had been hoping to hear, and not totally unexpected.

"It would be good to work together again, like we did all those years ago," she replied, trying to sound excited.

Her plan was to send her sister off to be caught by the hunter, while she set about finding out what game Alkira was playing, and what The Council were up to. If that meant there was an opportunity to get rid of them, all the better. Unfortunately, her sister would be far more interested in the idea of getting rid of The Council, and would be keen on doing that part herself. She would have to make the job of going after the bow-and-arrow man sound more exciting than it really was, and then persuade her sister that she would be better suited to doing that instead.

"Well, there are two things. I believe The Council are playing some kind of game. Everyone wants to get rid of them so maybe this is our chance," she said.

Jackie's eyes twinkled at the thought of that. She opened her mouth to speak, and began to raise her hand for a high-five.

"No! Nothing like that!", said Jennifer. "Something a bit less, er, violent. They're not really bad people, they're just useless."

"And stupid, and demented, and ridiculous. Or so I'm told."

"You really don't like them, do you?" observed Jennifer.

"Does it show that much?"

"Yes Jackie, it does, but what happens if we get rid of them?"

"We'll need a new structure. It won't work if there's nothing to take their place. A power vacuum is always dangerous. Someone or something will jump in and take over, and it almost certainly won't be what we want."

"It has to be other Aylas. No-one else knows enough to run things properly."

"Yeah. We can worry about that later though. Plenty of people will want to do it," observed Jackie, kicking the remains of an old burnt stick back into the fire pit.

Jennifer knew that was true. Plenty of people would want to do it, but mostly for the wrong reasons. The idea of being the master was appealing, but the purpose of a council was to serve as well as lead. They would have to find genuine people who cared about their job and were willing to take responsibility for their actions. Too many people thought that they could do whatever they liked, and when it went wrong they could find someone else to blame. They thought they were better than everyone else. They thought they were Very Important People. That was the problem. As far as she was concerned there was no such thing as a Very Important

Person. There were people who held Very Important Jobs, but the people themselves weren't very important. They were replaceable in an instant.

She had to admit that having a VIJ sounded like some kind of disease. It didn't sound half as appealing as being a VIP, but they could worry about that later.

"Okay," agreed Jennifer, with a smile. Even though she wanted to paint the job of going after The Council as boring, now was not the time to try engaging her sister in philosophical discussions about the merits of various traits to be considered in the selection of effective leaders. "We'll worry about that later," she said. "But the other more important task is to go and neutralise this destroyer-of-worlds."

"One of us could go after the creature, and the other could stay here and work on getting rid of The Council," said Jackie brightly.

Jennifer considered that in silence. It was, of course, exactly what she had wanted her sister to say.

The Council were useless at what they did, and most of them wouldn't be able to fight their way out of a wet paper bag, but if they heard about any plots to overthrow them, they could make what remained of your life very miserable, and extremely painful.

They had some formidable guards.

Jackie was looking at her with an air of expectation, as if watching the wheels turning as her sister worked it through in her head.

And that was exactly right, thought Jennifer after a moment or two. Following The Council's failed attempts to destroy the bow-and-arrow man, the words were better repeated with the emphasis on the past tense.

They *had* some formidable guards.

"I'm up for that," replied Jennifer.

As she had expected, Jackie thought the best idea was for her to stay behind and deal with The Council, while Jennifer went back to the twisted land looking for the creature.

"Why?" asked Jennifer.

"Because you know where it is, you've seen it."

"Mmmm, yes, I know. But that's the issue isn't it."

"What?"

"Did it know I was there? Did it see me? I don't think it did, but we can't know that for sure."

"I don't know anything about it though?" complained Jackie. "I don't even know what it looks like!"

"No, but I can tell you what I found out, and show you where to go."

"But if it had seen you, it would recognise me too."

"Yes," countered Jennifer. "But there's something we can do about that."

"And you? If you stay here, you don't know anything about The Council, so how does that help?"

Jennifer thought hard for a moment. She had an answer for that too.

"That's not a problem. I can always go and find out about The Council. Besides, all my worlds are here," she said firmly. "I won't leave them."

Jackie began to open her mouth, but Jennifer jumped in before she could speak.

"...and no, you couldn't look after them for me!"

"I have worlds that need looking after too y'know," replied Jackie, now sounding affronted.

Yes, thought Jennifer, and we could probably give a baboon a piece of rock and some bananas, and they'd be better worlds when it had finished scribbling, and rubbing its bottom on them.

If what she believed was in fact correct, the creature needed satisfying, and she couldn't bring herself to do that. Her plan would mean losing her sister forever, but that was for the best. Jackie wasn't really cut out for being a creator, that was the problem, so giving her up to the hunter was the right thing to do. It was a sacrifice that had to be made.

What did Jackie need to hear to convince her to go? Not the truth. She would never go if she knew the truth.

"Don't worry," she said, putting her arm around her sister's shoulder and giving her a squeeze. "I'll find someone to look after your worlds for a while. I'm sure this is a creature that you'll understand, and you'll be much better at dealing with it than I would be."

Jackie sighed, and seemed to accept the compliment.

Her sister had put forward a good argument, which was difficult to disagree with. Although she really wanted to stay here and go after The Council herself, she would play along for a bit and see what happened. After all, it couldn't do any harm.

Jennifer sat in silence, studying the cold, empty fire pit.

It was amazing what people would do for you if you told them what they wanted to hear.

The Marlow family had fallen apart after their father had gone off on one of his adventures and never returned. That had been the beginning of the end for Jennifer and her sister. He loved his daughters more than anything else in the world, and he would never have abandoned them, so something must have happened to him. He was either dead, or had been unable to come home. She had often walked hand-in-hand with him when they went off hiking in the hills, and he had always promised he would take her with him on some 'proper' adventures when she was older. She missed him so very much, and getting her nose down to the grindstone and building a career as a respected Creator of Worlds had been her way of surviving. It was a double blow when she'd fallen out so spectacularly with her sister, and lost her to another world as well. After that she had lived for her work. There was always the chance that her father would turn up one day, but as time went on it became increasingly less likely. The only other possibility of rebuilding any of her past family life would have been to rekindle her relationship with Jackie. Now she had apparently done that, but it wasn't going to last. Jackie had to go away again, forever this time, to another world to find her destiny, and then all hope of ever being part of a family again would be lost.

It would not be getting dark for a while, so there were still a few hours left to reminisce.

"Let's spend a bit of time here and talk about old times," said Jennifer sadly, "and then I'll take you to the other world and explain what I've discovered."

13 - A New Adventure

"Okay, keep hold of me here because it's still slippery where the car went over the edge."

Jennifer was holding Jackie's hand, and leading her across the ground towards the rocky ledge overlooking the river.

She hadn't had any problem recalling the time and place where they needed to be. It had to be after the girl had been rescued, and after she'd been to the town and sat in the bus shelter to return home. The following day was fine. She wouldn't have been able to go to that world while she was still there of course. That just wasn't possible, and it would be a silly idea anyway.

Jackie was looking at the wheel tracks, and the broken saplings.

"So, the car went over here?" she asked, pointing at the edge.

"Yes," replied Jennifer. "With the man in it that I think must have been her father. They both had a similar kind of aura. The girl had dark hair and she was quite small. About six or seven years old I'd guess."

"What's her name?" asked Jackie.

"I have no idea. I never talked to her."

Jennifer had brought them there in the late evening, which had given them a chance to look around before the light had begun to fade. Now that night was starting to close in it would be easier to find their way to the other time where the rescue took place.

"I think it's better to take you there than to try giving you the memory of where it is," said Jennifer, closing her eyes and beginning to recall the columns of smoke that drifted upwards from the glowing fires, the clouds and the sky, and the smell of the air and the noises of the forest.

Jackie took her hand, although she probably didn't need to. It was just a convention, a protocol. It meant "I'm ready", although Jennifer was going anyway, and they were stood so close that it wouldn't have mattered. It was easier when you were taking a cooperative willing soul with you, rather than an unconscious dying life form, a bunch of rocks, and apparently, an invisible bow-and-arrow man.

They didn't manage to emerge in exactly the same place and time, because the memories she had of the rescue involved a world where she would have already existed, so it required a bit of mental jiggery pokery in order to find a time in which she was able to exist again without being in the same place twice. That was always an uncomfortable feeling, being halfway between worlds and finding nowhere to be solid again, especially when you had someone with you who could exist perfectly well there, and you couldn't. You just had to make sure you didn't drop them, because you wouldn't be able to go back and pick them up. Having said that, it wouldn't have mattered much if she'd dropped Jackie. Her sister was perfectly capable of finding her way around by herself, and wouldn't have remained lost for long, but that wasn't the point.

After a few seconds, when the last remaining patches of the world had stopped being translucent and everything had solidified, they set off down the steep slope towards the plain.

From what Jennifer could tell, it felt like it was the evening after the settlers had rescued the girl. There were outlines of various animals around, but no red or orange-tinged ones that could have been the bow-and-arrow man. In fact, Jennifer noted, there was nothing human sized at all.

She was trying to work out where they were on the plain from the map she had in her head of what it had looked like from the ridge. The tracks they were walking were becoming more defined now, so these were well used. By her reckoning, the rescuers had come from the settlement which was ahead of them and to the left, further away from the hills.

Jackie was tagging along behind, cursing and limping now and again as she caught her ankle on some bit of scrub, or put her foot down awkwardly on a rock.

"You'll get the hang of it eventually," said Jennifer, just loud enough to be heard. "It's an acquired skill."

That didn't seem to satisfy her sister at all.

The settlement was bigger than Jennifer had imagined it would be. Around the perimeter, forming a circle, were about a dozen wooden huts with thatched roofs made from brush. A fire burned in the middle and some washing hung nearby.

People were milling about, clutching bowls and pans. That meant they had access to metalworkers, she thought. Perhaps they got them from visiting traders, they didn't look to have big enough fires and workshops to make goods like that themselves.

There were twenty or thirty people here, but where was the girl?

Jennifer couldn't see her. There were a few other children, but not the girl she had arranged for them to rescue the previous night. Maybe she had died after all, or was still badly injured in one of the huts.

Then, through the flickering flames of the fire, she saw a face. A small figure sitting in a doorway on the other side of the circle, holding a bowl. The boy who had been carrying the stick was there too, further in the hut where it was harder to see details.

"That's her, over there," whispered Jennifer, pointing across through the flames.

Jackie looked along her arm.

"She seems to be alright."

"Well, she's survived, and they're looking after her because she's got food in that bowl," replied Jennifer.

"But no creature," said Jackie.

"No, it's not here. It was definitely a man. Young, with dark curly hair and a rugged face."

"And you're sure he had the aura?"

"Absolutely," replied Jennifer. "Quite distinctive. You'll know him as soon as you see him."

"Maybe he's gone somewhere else now though," said Jackie. "Perhaps to another world?"

Jennifer seemed hesitant.

"No, I don't think so," she answered eventually. "And even if he has, he'll be back, I'm sure about that."

***

After observing the settlers for a while, and deciding that there was nothing more to learn, they began to walk back along the path towards the hills.

"So that's what I found out about the creature," said Jennifer. "It seems a fairly straightforward and simple existence here, so..."

"Whoaaa!" squeaked Jackie, looking around herself as if something had stung her.

"What?"

"Just back there. We walked through something! Didn't you feel it?"

"No," admitted Jennifer, stopping dead in her tracks. "I wasn't really paying attention."

Jackie turned her face towards the sky. That was always the first place to look for changes. It didn't look any different. Neither did the surroundings, although in the dark it was difficult to tell.

"It felt like we walked into another world."

Jennifer shrugged.

"Well, I didn't do it. I wasn't even thinking about anywhere else."

They took each other's hands. Not out of any deep fear or concern, it was just a normal reaction when faced with something that felt odd. It meant that, no matter what either of them did, or thought, or whatever happened, they couldn't get split up. They both had to finish up in the same place and time.

It wasn't unknown for worlds to exhibit strange behaviour, just uncommon, a bit like turning a corner and experiencing a sudden gust of wind when it had been quite calm. Unexpected, that was all.

They took a few more steps, side by side.

"There!" said Jackie. "Happened again. Did you feel it?"

Jennifer sighed.

"I'm not sure. Something didn't feel right, and it still doesn't, but nothing I can put my finger on."

"Let's go back just a little way," replied Jackie.

They both turned around to face in the opposite direction, and swapped hands. It was easier than walking round in a circle.

"Somewhere... here," said Jackie after a few careful steps.

"No. I don't feel anything."

"Me neither."

"Okay," muttered Jennifer. "Let's just get out of here. It doesn't feel very stable."

The girls turned around to face the way they had been going, and took a step.

"Oh, but now the path is different!" exclaimed Jackie.

It was, and so was the sky. The ground underfoot was damp and felt as if it had more grass growing on it, and the sky was brighter, with no moon but fewer clouds and more stars. It wasn't frightening, just worrying because whenever you moved to strange and unknown worlds, you needed to be prepared to take a very good look around, to make sure you were safe and not about to be sprung on by some hungry predator. When it just happened without warning that was a big problem because you never knew what you had walked into.

"I think," said Jennifer very carefully, "that we should take ourselves straight back to the rocky ledge from here, without trying to go any further."

Jackie agreed, but it proved to be easier said than done. Jennifer found that visualising the time and place in her mind was easy. For some reason it was just difficult to go there. The first time she opened her eyes they were both still standing in the same place. The second time there was nothing there, just featureless blackness in all directions. After a bit of extra concentration, it worked on the third try.

They sat on a boulder in the shade for a rest, and to consider what had happened. These symptoms were well known. When you drew worlds too close to each other, or you let them expand until their boundaries began to overlap, they bumped into each other, and life got very confusing. If the worlds that collided were very similar the inhabitants might just wake up somewhere slightly different one morning and think they'd had a bad night on the town, but if they were very different, life could get scary for them. The worlds on the wall of the cave were just a jumbled mess, so it wasn't surprising they were highly unpredictable.

"What do we do now?" asked Jackie. "And why is that girl important anyway?"

Jennifer had an answer to the first question, but not the second.

"You need to stay here, and keep tracking that man," she said, and I need to go back right now and try to work out a plan to get rid of The Council."

Jackie was waiting for the answer to the second question.

"I don't know why the girl is important," said Jennifer. "I was going to leave her to die, but the world wanted me to rescue her. I suspect she has some part to play, but right now I don't know what it is."

114

They were both used to worlds wanting something. It was just one of those odd characteristics of them. Once you had complex life, it developed a collective consciousness of its own. The complex creatures were individuals, but they were made up of smaller organisms like cells that were also individuals in their own right. The thoughts of the collections of organisms overpowered the thoughts of the individual ones, but the dust from which they were all made still had a life of its own.

That was what formed first, when new life was developing. A web of living dust that spread across the entire world. First the tinges of colour, then the simple life, which gathered around the templates to make complex creatures. Nobody understood exactly how the world wide web worked, and it was unpredictable, but it did work, it had a mind of its own, and if it really wanted something done you could never fight it for long because it was everywhere.

"So, you need to see that no harm comes to her," said Jennifer sternly. The expression on her sister's face led her to believe Jackie wasn't convinced. She reached into her pocket and pulled out one of the notebooks that she'd found in the trunk. "This is for you," she said, holding it out for her sister to take.

Jackie turned the little book over in her hands a couple of times. It was carefully bound in soft purple leather, with a space down the spine for a pencil, which was still there.

"What's this?" she asked, with a tinge of derision in her voice.

"You know how Dad was always keeping logs of his travels and adventures," Jennifer replied. "He said that a notebook was important because it not only gave others a chance to benefit from the things you achieved in your life, but also gave *you* the opportunity to look back on your journey and become a better person."

"Yeah," said Jackie, sadly.

"When we were young, he bought us both notebooks with our names in them. This is yours. I kept it when the house was cleared out. He would have wanted you to have it."

"He never told me," replied her sister, now squeezing the little book more affectionately.

"I think he was keeping them for the day he could take us with him on his big adventures," said Jennifer softly. "But you are off on a big adventure of your own now. I know you can read and write much better than me. You should write it all down, so it will never be forgotten."

Her sister opened the book carefully.

'To Jacqueline with Love' was inscribed on the inside cover, in her father's best handwriting. Jackie chuckled. He had always liked to call his daughters Jennifer and Jacqueline. Her sister was happy with that, and had kept using her full name. It had worked for her, and still did, but Jacqueline had always sounded too, well, posh and stuck-up. And of course, she hadn't gone by the name Marlow for a long time, it was somehow too closely associated with her smart-arse sister, but the initials JM still worked for her as Jackie Morrison.

"And we'll keep in touch?" she asked.

"Yes, of course. We can work out the details once we've both found out more about what is happening, but for a start let's meet back here in a week's time."

"Yep. Sounds good to me."

Jennifer picked up a small stone with a tinge of lichen on it.

"I'll put this on top of that log over there when I come back to meet you, so if you imagine this scene with me sitting here and the stone in place, that will give you your time marker."

"Okay. That works. I suppose," replied Jackie hesitantly, glancing up at the tree canopy to memorise the shape of the branches better. It would be easy to find her way back here,

116

or to simply go home if she wanted. It hadn't worked out the way she'd expected, but she would at least make an effort, and then she'd be able to persuade her sister to swap with her after their meeting when she'd found out more.

"But you can't go back still looking like you do now," said Jennifer, slipping the little stone into her pocket while her sister wasn't looking. "Especially now we know the whole world is broken. Even if he didn't see me originally there's no knowing whether the creature has seen us or not with all the gaps and disparities we've encountered."

Jackie looked across at her with a very concerned expression.

"So, what am I supposed to do?" she said.

This was the bit that Jennifer hadn't been looking forward to. If her suppositions were correct, the plan would only work if Jackie was an adult, but there was no way she could tell her that. It would only work if Jackie didn't know what she was letting herself in for.

"I can imagine it won't be pleasant, but you need to consider reversing what we did all those years ago, and go back there looking like an adult, or at least an older girl."

Jackie gave her the side-eye.

"Really! You expect me to go shape-shifting again!"

Jennifer felt uncomfortable. It was time to go, before it turned into an argument. This wasn't how she'd imagined she would eventually say goodbye to her sister. She took one long last look at Jackie, closed her eyes, and began to think of home.

"Life is going to be unnecessarily difficult if you meet up with the bow-and-arrow man looking like a little girl," she said, as she felt the world around her slowly disappearing.

After she had gone, Jackie sat for a long time, staring at the space where her sister had been sitting, and listening to the rustling of the leaves until the faint traces of her outline had disappeared completely.

That was Jennifer for you, she thought. She always wins, and you don't realise until it's too late.

14 - The Visit

Jennifer took some big breaths of warm air.

City air, that's what it was.

Not the kind of cool, fresh air that smelled and tasted of agriculture, but used air that smelled of food and people, and drains. From her vantage point on the bridge halfway across the river it was still picturesque though. The silhouettes of old buildings against the darkening blue sky with the street lamps twinkling off the ripples in the water would make a good memory. If all went as planned tonight, she might well want to return to this place in the future.

There were things she needed to know, and that involved getting close to The Council. Not too close though, just close enough to watch and listen.

They were supposed to meet in secret, but word of mouth was a wonderful thing, and plenty of people had been willing to speak about groups of Aylas holding mysterious meetings.

Having identified the appropriate world, all Jennifer had needed to do was find the right place. Enquiries at the local shop had proved fruitful and had also revealed that the little collective met every week. Every week! That seemed often for a council, but then these were dangerous times, she told herself. They must have a full agenda and a lot to do, she thought.

The place she believed they met was just across the road on the south bank of the river. The old stone buildings there were constructed against the side of a steep hill, so they had no sky behind them and weren't so pretty to look at. People should be turning up very soon, if her information was correct. She scanned the path carefully for signs of life.

Not many people were around considering it was a warm night, and the local tavern had not long opened its doors to an empty street. The owner had turned on the outside lights to illuminate the sign which read **The Kafalonia Inn**, opened the door, and stepped outdoors to crank his awning down a little way. There wasn't any need for it, the sky didn't look like rain, but it caught the lights and made the front of the building look more inviting. She knew she needed to remember all these details, on the assumption that she might want to return to this place and time one day.

A shape which had the aura of an old man sauntered up the road and disappeared into a small brown doorway just along from the tavern. She was expecting to see Aylas, so maybe that wasn't the place after all.

At various intervals along the front of the building were gratings which took up the full width of the path. Jennifer knew what they were, she'd seen them in other places. They were big drains, deep vertical shafts that joined up beneath the road, where they emptied flood water from the hill into the river, so it didn't pour across the road and wash it away when there were big storms. There weren't going to be any of those tonight though, she thought. The sky didn't look like rain.

Across the mouth of the river, out towards the edge of the world, Jennifer watched the sun shimmer and boil away into the sea, toasting the bottom of the clouds with an orange glow which slowly faded into greyness. That was how it appeared anyway, but it was just an illusion caused by the world turning. Her world was certainly turning, that was for sure, and nothing was ever quite the way it seemed. What Alkira had told her wasn't the truth, she knew that now. The bow-and-arrow man would be satisfied if it caught her sister. She was the key to getting rid of it, whether she knew it or not, but the council was another matter entirely. She needed to get into their world, or at least find out exactly what went on, because that might give her the information she needed to fit more of the puzzle together. It was also likely that some members of the council were also disillusioned with it, and that would hopefully provide her with access to some like-minded conspirators who would prove invaluable when the time came to restructure the organisation.

After a while, as the sky grew darker, her patience was rewarded. Over a period of about ten minutes, several figures with orange outlines appeared from various directions and made their way through the door. Nobody seemed to notice her.

Jennifer set off carefully towards the row of buildings.

It was time to stop looking nonchalant and find a surreptitious way in.

***

In the stone hall with its vaulted roof, Number One cleared her throat.

"Now then, to the subject of the imminent threat from the destroyer of worlds," she began. "I trust that you have all read my report, which you will find on page two of the document in front of you."

There followed a shuffling of papers as various members searched for page two, and others attempted to dislodge crumbs and bits of cake from it.

"Oooh, yes!" muttered Number Four. "I see our new agent is ill."

"I'm sorry?" said Number One.

"It says here she's sick."

Number One looked closely at the document in front of her, and fixed Number Four with a steely gaze.

"Here somewhere," said Number Four, pointing at the sheet with a wrinkly finger and moving her glasses up and down her nose as if it would make any difference. "Ah, yes, here. It says that Alkira said: "I have taken Jennifer to the place where we believed the threat was last seen, and she is dropped off [sic]".

Number One closed her eyes in despair.

It was Number Two who broke the silence.

"No! That doesn't mean she's ill."

"But it says so!"

"No! It says *sic*. That means that what was written is wrong."

"Then why wasn't it fixed?" croaked Number Three.

"Because that's what she said," replied Number Two. "It's a quote, and if it was fixed then it wouldn't be what she said, so it would be wrong."

"But you said it was wrong anyway!"

"Yes, but it has to be written wrong, because then it's right. If it was written right, it would be wrong."

"Sounds very silly to me," said Number Three.

"ANYWAY..." interjected Number One, in an attempt to get the subject back on track.

"So, she's not sick then?" said Number Four.

"NO," cried Number One in despair, now leaning on the table with both hands. "No-one is sick!"

"My granddaughter isn't very well," said Number Two, through a mouthful of crumbs.

Number One's hands were just beginning to clench into fists of rage, when the conversation was interrupted by the sound of metal tinkling on the stone floor.

"Now I've dropped my spoon," muttered Number Three.

"It's alright. I can get it," said Number Two, patting her soothingly on the hand.

"Never mind! You don't all need to read it. The essence of the report is that the new agent has been taken to the scene, and has likely made contact with the creature," said Number One.

"Has she come back?"

Number One thought about this momentarily.

"Not that we know of," she replied, "however…"

Her eye was drawn to a heaving mass which was apparently attempting to dig its way under the table.

She took a deep breath, followed by an equally big sigh.

"WHEN YOU HAVE COMPLETELY FINISHED…" she said, in the direction of the enormous bottom, "we can perhaps continue this discussion, which is, I might add, of utmost importance to the continuing safety and welfare of our entire society?"

There was a dull thud that shook the table, and the figure backed out slowly, knocking over the chair with a crash.

From the shadows in the gallery, Jennifer's little grubby face peered down at the scene with a terrified expression.

They had the unmistakable aura. They were definitely Aylas, which meant they would be able to see her if they happened to look up. They should really be able to sense her presence as well, she thought, but they'd just got old and demented.

There was nothing wrong with getting old and demented of course. Lots of people were old and demented, but they didn't try to rule the world.

At that moment, Jefferson appeared with another tray of cakes and more tea.

"About time!" scolded Number Three. "You really need to get a move on young man."

"Yes Ma'am," he muttered, before turning smartly about-face and heading back towards the kitchen door.

Jennifer had been determined to pay a visit to the meeting and see what it was all about, and what they did.

In retrospect, she was beginning to wish she hadn't.

Clearly they were a bunch of buffoons who were capable of nothing useful at all.

She had been hoping it might have been possible to 'turn' some of them, and perhaps reward them with a useful role in a future council, however it was clear that there was nothing of value here. Except perhaps the leader. She seemed pretty switched on and showed promise, but an established leader would almost certainly not want to be anything except the head of a new council, and that wasn't going to happen.

It wasn't possible to see who they all were, the masques they wore were effective at a distance, and she wouldn't have wanted to get too close or try to follow any of them. There was no shortage of Aylas around these parts and she couldn't hide from people who were able to see her distinctive aura. Townsfolk had been willing to talk to her when she was looking for the meeting place. They would be just as willing to talk to anyone else who happened to ask around about other suspicious activities. Talk was cheap, and gossip was cheaper.

It didn't matter who they were anyway, there was clearly nobody in the existing council who could be employed in a useful capacity.

They would all have to go, and that needed a new plan.

One seat around the table had been empty tonight, which meant someone was missing, and Alkira was clearly working for them. That was very interesting and confirmed some of her suspicions. She needed to find out more about this bunch of buffoons, but it wasn't a sensible idea to try following Aylas.

That was a problem that didn't take much solving though, there was always a way around everything.

Not everyone at the meeting was an Ayla.

***

By the time she had left the building by the service door at the back the night had settled in. The street lamps were out, the tavern was closed and the world was dark and silent. All but one person had already gone home. She would wait just around the corner until her intended target left the building by the brown door opposite the bridge, and then follow at a respectable distance.

She waited, listening for the sound of movement. Eventually she heard the door open, and the rattle of keys as it was closed again and locked. She peered carefully around the corner. The figure was walking away from her, as she had expected. That was the direction it had originally come from. With a bit of stealth there was no chance it would be aware of her from this distance.

She raised herself up to her full height, took a deep breath, grabbed hold of a drainpipe, and swung herself around the corner into the evening mist to follow it.

***

Back at home, drops of rain trickled their way down the vines that covered the end of the tunnel, where they dripped off the ends into the concrete chute and began their journey to a different life. The sky rumbled, and Jennifer held on to her mug of warm tea a bit more tightly. Home was home, whether it was sunny or stormy, and at least it was safe here.

When she had set out on this challenge it had sounded straightforward. The mission was simple: Get rid of the bow-and-arrow creature. It had begun well, but then most things did. Most people set out with good intentions. That didn't mean that what they were trying to do would ultimately work, or be a good thing even if it did.

The hard work at the cave had led her to a couple of revealing conclusions. The patches of broken worlds had been hastily smudged together, probably as soon as the symbol for the bow-and-arrow man had been drawn in one of them. There were sweeps and arcs and lines where the drawings had been rubbed in circles. The marks all fitted the radius you would expect from a wrist and joints in an arm. She had measured them, and they were all from the same arm. The destroyer of the worlds in the cave had been one person with a wet cloth. Someone about the same size as she was.

After doing all her calculations she had gone looking for a well-deserved rest, and what she had found, or rather *not* found, had added to the puzzle. In a small recess at the back of the cave was the remains of a bed with no mattress, a rusty bucket, and a few old pots lying upside-down in the dust. There was nowhere to sleep or cook. Nobody had lived in that cave for years.

What she had read in her father's book had provided the final piece of the jigsaw.

The book had said the hunter that arose as a result of drawing the bow-and-arrow symbol was inextricably bound to the Ayla who drew it. But the hunter had seemed receptive to *her* mind, and the world Alkira had taken her to thought she was its creator.

There was no doubt now that her suspicions were correct. Her identical twin sister, Jackie, must have drawn those hastily scribbled worlds, put the bow-and-arrow symbol in them, and then smudged them all together to make it look as if the creature had destroyed them. That was why there was nowhere to live in the cave.

Jackie was the one the hunter really wanted, not her.

It had been somewhat difficult persuading her to go after it, but Jackie had never been cut out to be an Ayla. Her work was too avant-garde, too Bohemian, too mad quite frankly, and she'd never cared about the worlds she'd created, which was shamefully disrespectful to their inhabitants. On top of all that she was a somewhat deeply troubled girl, and never truly happy with her life. Creating worlds was not the right job for her. Both Jackie, and the universe, would be better off if she fell prey to the hunter. That was why Jennifer had felt she had to harden her heart. She'd made that choice. It hadn't been an easy one.

And then there was the incident with the car. Some people would have put it down to pure coincidence, but Jennifer had dealt with enough worlds to know otherwise. A car appearing from around a bend on a rainy night with a windscreen covered in rain and the driver momentarily distracted, just as she happened to step into the road was not a coincidence. That world hated its creator enough to want her dead.

Apparently, it wasn't only boys that were unable to tell them apart.

At least the first piece of her plan was working out. Jackie was in the twisted land with the hunter, where she belonged, and she wasn't planning to go back for her.

The problem now was The Council. She had suspicions about that too. For a start, Alkira had not been here looking after her worlds, as promised, but also it was clear that she was involved in something much more sinister. It was likely that Jackie fitted in with it all somehow, but right at the moment she didn't have any proof.

Jennifer reached down and rubbed the graze on her knee, an injury which she had picked up during her quest to follow the old man on the previous evening. Perhaps holding on to the drainpipe had helped a little to avoid disaster when she had swung herself around the corner outside the meeting hall into the mist, but experienced Aylas never lost the habits of a lifetime. She regularly came face-to-face with death in many worlds, but whoever had lifted up the stormwater grating that night was mistaken to assume that anyone with a knack for staying alive would swing around a corner without looking where they were putting their feet.

The conclusion was inescapable: Somebody else wanted her dead as well.

She could worry about that later, but the priority right now was to make sure Jackie stayed with the hunter. Once her sister realised that she hadn't turned up to the rendezvous, she would either think that Jennifer was in trouble, or would conclude she'd been abandoned there.

Either way, she would try to come back and cause trouble.

There was only one way to make sure she couldn't.

To Jacqueline with Love

Here's hoping your life is full of adventures

Dad
XXX

~~ 1 ~~

Day 3

I've spent the last two days messing about on the plain looking for the girl and the hunter, but there's no trace of them, so I thought I'd start making these stupid notes just in case something happens to me.

Just for the record, this job is a pain. It's not what I had in mind at all. Jennifer should be out here doing all this instead of staying behind in the comfort of home going after five old women.

My mobile phone doesn't work, there's nowhere to hang out, no shops, no-one to talk to, nowhere to get a coffee, and no way to keep warm. I am NOT going to try changing back to being an adult. It's a ridiculous thing to do and I've no idea why she thinks I would ever want to. I feel much less conspicuous like this, and anyway, even if I succeeded in going back to being an adult, I'd have no clothes that fit me.

There's no sign of either the girl or the hunter anywhere, but the sky looks consistently different from day to day across in the distance, so the world might be different over there.

I need to find a place to stay, so I'm gonna hide somewhere again tonight, and set off across the plain tomorrow to see if there's any sign of them in that direction.

It's cold here because the sky is very clear in this world when there are no clouds. Hopefully I will find somewhere warm to sleep again tonight without being discovered by any groups of settlers. If I find someplace dark, I can manage to blend into the surroundings, and no-one will see my shape in the shadows. That has worked the last couple of nights, but I don't sleep well when I'm not solidly rooted in any one existence.

Jennifer seems better at it than I am. Perhaps because she goes away to other worlds all the time. I'm not used to this.
Maybe she thinks I need the practice or something.

~~ 2 ~~

Day 4

I found a place to sleep overnight underneath a bush behind a hut in one of the settlements. It was cold but some warmth drifted across from the remains of a nearby fire. I didn't have to disappear much to blend in, so I slept better than I have on previous nights.

This morning was bright and warm, with a deep blue sky full of puffy little white clouds, so walking the tracks was pleasant.

I thought the plain would be bigger than it really was. It probably only took me an hour to walk right across it. From a distance it looked huge until I started walking it, and then all of a sudden it seemed so much more manageable. I guess life is like that too. We all think it will be big, and then once we start walking through it, all of a sudden we find ourselves at the end, and we don't know where the time went.

I found an old railway line along the top of an embankment at the far side. It hasn't been used for a long time, and a lot of the rails and sleepers have been taken, probably to build things with.

There's an arch made of granite blocks, which goes underneath it. That'll save me having to climb up the embankment to get over the line in future. I'm grubby enough as it is, and I've ripped some of my clothes already. They won't last forever and I've no idea where I'll be able to get any more, which is another reason I need to go home.

There's a long strip of forest on the other side of the railway that stretches for miles, trapped between the embankment and an old twisty river, and that world is different. The forest is denser, and everything is green and lush, but more importantly, I now have a temporary home because I found a little room with a domed roof built into the stone archway, that looks like it was once used to store tools and stuff for maintaining the railway. The iron door was rusted shut, but I managed to prise it open with a lump of wood, and it's quite comfortable inside. It goes down a few steps into the ground, so it's built into the foundations.

It's cold at night but I've made a bed of dry grass which I can dig myself into, so I'm staying here until tomorrow, and will go off exploring again in the morning. At least I'll be safe and won't need to keep one eye open all night in case something thinks I'm edible.

~~ 3 ~~

Day 5

The little room was surprisingly comfortable.
It made a change from hiding during the day and
skulking about in the evenings on the lookout for
the outlines of dangerous creatures, but I still don't
function properly unless I've had a coffee.

I expect I'll get over it.

I'm still hating this idea. All I want is to find the
bow-and-arrow thing, work out what we need to
do to destroy it, and then find the girl and go
home.

I'm sure I'll be able to free up the door to the room
a bit and make it shut properly, and it'll be even
better if I can get the handle to turn on the inside
so it locks.

I went under the railway today, to explore the
forest in the long strip of land on the river side of
the embankment as planned. It feels much safer
than the area on the plain because I can walk
about without falling through holes into other
worlds, and it's warmer. I don't know why.

There's something odd about going under the arch through the embankment from one side to the other. It's like a gateway between two very different worlds, and they somehow feel like they're in different times as well. It's a kind of fracture. This is not something I've ever experienced before, at least not as big and obvious as this. Something very strange is happening here and I don't know what it is.

I spent the morning walking downstream on a path along the riverbank. It's a bit muddy and it seems to go on forever, and there are a few places that feel a bit wobbly, but nowhere near as treacherous as the plain between the embankment and the hills where I was searching before.

There's nothing I can find to eat here, so I'm either going to have to go back to a settlement and try to steal food, or catch something and make a fire, but I've got no easy way to do either of those things at the moment.

I've broken most of my fingernails already and I haven't even been here a week.

4

Day 6

I spent the day around the arch today, just
exploring and making the place decent.

There are fewer paths here and they all look like
animal tracks, but no-one from the settlements
seems to come as far as the railway embankment. I
wonder if it might be too difficult for them to get
back home again. Maybe if they come here they get
lost, so they've learned not to venture off the plain.

I found a rusty tin with some old oil in it under a
pile of rubbish near the railway line and got the
door handle to turn by oiling it and hitting it
with a stick, so now the door can be latched shut,
but I'm filthy now, and smelly.

I tried to have a wash in the river but fell in and
got soaked.
I don't know how anyone manages to survive
outside like this.

A few berries grow around the area, although it's
not clear how the seasons work, so I don't
understand how things can grow properly. I ate
some of them and I'm not dead yet.

Sometimes I go back to the same place and there aren't any, which just goes to show that time, or something, is clearly messed up around here.

Even if I could light a fire it would attract attention and I've nothing to cook on it, and I don't need a fire to keep warm because the little room seems cosy.

I've never noticed beautiful skies before. I'm sure we had them in the city. There's something kinda relaxing about looking up at the sky.

The evening ones are especially picturesque here. There's usually a yellow moon hiding behind layers of thin cloud. You'd think it shouldn't happen that often, but it does.

At the end of the day, when I'm tired and it's getting too gloomy to do anything, it's somehow nice to just lay on the embankment and gaze up at the fading light.

5

Day 7

I'm starving today. I'm not dying, but I feel like I ought to be. I've not found anywhere with cell signal, but I've been using my phone as a flashlight over the past few nights, so the battery is dead anyway.

This afternoon I went off in the opposite direction along the river, which is upstream, where I found a little house in a clearing behind a rise, where it couldn't be seen from the path. I never expected to find anything like that. It's out of place, as if it belongs in another world and a kid just dropped it there.

It's the sort of little house you'd expect to see on a picture postcard, or in a fairy story, and someone is living in it because there's smoke coming out of the chimney. So far, I've not seen anyone go in or out though. I hope it doesn't have three bears and bowls of porridge in it. It looks like it ought to, at least from the outside anyway.

There's another structure in the clearing too. A strange wooden tower, like a lighthouse, painted white.

I've no idea what it's for or who made it, but it's pretty old and bits of it look like they're falling off. I really want to have a closer look at it, but I need to suss out the area better first.

Whoever lives in the house must have food, but I'm not willing to go charging in until I know what's happening, so I'm going to stay here and watch until I find out whether it's safe or not. I've found a place to hide in some bushes around the back of the old tower where I can still see the house, but hopefully no-one can see me. It's a bit warmer here in the denser forest than it was on the exposed plain, so I'll stay here tonight. Going back to the little room to keep warm is not so important. Finding food is.

I'm tired but I need to keep an eye out for any occupants of the house. I'll be able to relax a bit more here because I've seen no predators around this area, so maybe I can sleep a bit better here and not be on edge all the time.

6

Day 7

I fell asleep without even putting this notebook back in my pocket yesterday evening. That's how tired I was, but I was woken up later in the night by someone with a distinctive aura returning to the house. It went in the front door, which didn't appear to be locked. It was obviously the hunter from the reddish colours in its outline, but it had a human feel to it too.

That's a coincidence. Of all the places it could have been, I just happened to come across it here.

When it got light, a girl came out with some washing and hung it on a line. This has to be the girl that Jennifer rescued. I was right in thinking time was different here because she's grown up now, late teens, maybe early twenties. That's a big shift in time, caused I think by going through the archway — or maybe the worlds are really scrambled up.

During the day, another girl appeared as well. I first saw her through a window, moving about inside, but then she came out into the clearing and lit a fire, which they cooked on later in the evening after most of the flames had died down . I didn't see anyone else, so it looks like the hunter and two girls live here. It's easy to tell them apart because the other girl has very long blonde hair.

I'm sure the dark-haired girl called the hunter Sam, and he called her what sounded like Carrie. If she was about six at the time of the car crash, as Jennifer thought, she would remember her name. So that's probably her proper and original name.

I haven't heard anyone call the blonde girl by her name yet.

I'm starving and I'm still filthy, and I've torn even more of my clothes on the bushes climbing up and down embankments.

I know he's supposed to be a destroyer of worlds, but he doesn't look especially dangerous, and he lives with two young girls who he hasn't killed yet, so I've made up my mind. They all look friendly enough, so I'm going to wait until it gets dark, when I'll be able to make an easier escape if I need to, and then go and see if they'll give me any food.

~~ 7 ~~

~~Day 8~~ Day 9

So, I went and scratched on the door last night.
No, wait. It was the night before last. This is Day
9. I've been here two days.

I wasn't exactly made welcome, but I wasn't rejected
either, and it quickly became apparent that
another pair of hands to help with work wasn't
going to meet with disapproval.

I really felt uncomfortable at first, and had to
come to a quick decision, which was that I wasn't
going to try talking to them.

Firstly, I've nothing to say, but also, I dunno how to
explain anything to them. The two girls are
human beings, the destroyer-of-worlds is a tertiary
creature of some kind, and I'm a creator of worlds.
What could I say to them? I can't explain why I'm
here. I came to kill the bow-and-arrow creature,
which is the one they call Sam. I have a feeling
that wouldn't go down well.

The truth isn't good enough, so I'd have to make
something up and it wouldn't be long before I got
caught out, especially as they spend a lot of time

having conversations, usually by the fire. I've decided not to speak at all and remain mysterious.

There's no obvious way to get rid of him and I've had enough of trying to understand what's happening here. It's a totally screwed up world and it doesn't look like he's trying to destroy it at all — it's more like he's somehow trying to fix it.

Tonight, if I can get away without attracting attention, I'll return to the rendezvous point with the information I've gathered, and then Jennifer can come and sort this out.

I've had enough.

Day 10

Last night I tried to return to the rendezvous spot, where there ought to be a lichen-covered stone on top of the log, and there I expected to find my sister.

Even though time may not run at the same rate in all these twisted lands, at least a week should have passed in the world where she left me, so there ought to be a time when she is sat there waiting.

There is no place like that which I can travel to, so it doesn't exist, and therefore never has and never will. It's as if she has never gone back there to meet me. There is also no connection to my apartment, or her home in the tunnels. I can imagine them very clearly, but they don't exist.

It's as if there is no path back to the world I came from. Perhaps, somehow, this fractured set of worlds is shielding everything from the outside universe. It doesn't matter if I go back under the railway to the plain, or through any of the discontinuities between worlds here in the area near the river. There's still no connection to any other familiar world.

For the moment, I will take the optimistic view that the paths to the edges of this twisted mess are so convoluted that there is just no visibility of what lies outside it. That means I need to start mapping it in some way so I can learn my way around.

I'll start doing that tomorrow.

Right now it's dark, and the light from a little yellow crescent moon is breaking through the thin layer of clouds that roll out all the way to the horizon and reflecting from the ripples in the river. It's somehow soothing. I like it.

I'm stuck here for the moment, but at least I have food and a comfy place to live. Everyone seems friendly enough and the blonde girl, whose name is Tilly, gave me some clothes. They could fit me better but at least they're clean and not shredded. I don't know why, but I have a feeling they used to belong to her. I'm no good at estimating ages, but she looks as if she's in her late teens or early twenties, just like I was once.
If she has clothes here that now fit me that would mean she's been here for a long time.

There are no bears, or porridge.

17 - The Artist

Jennifer leaned on the edge of the cave entrance looking out across the desert sand dunes and feeling the warm wind blow gently across her face.

It had been a difficult decision, to send her sister away to be hunted down as prey, but sadly it was the only sensible solution.

The book had said that, amongst other things, when the bow-and-arrow symbol was drawn a destroyer-of-worlds would be created. That was probably where the whispered legends about it came from. Her sister had thought creating a destroyer-of-worlds sounded like a good idea, but when you were considering invoking a powerful and mysterious force it was usually a good idea to find and read *all* the instructions first.

Drops of muddy water dribbled from the tattered old piece of cloth she clutched tightly in her hand, and made ripples on the surface of the water in the bucket at her feet. A small piece of damp paper lay on the floor of the cave behind her.

She turned her head slowly to look back at the now featureless red sandstone wall.

There was no way out of those worlds for her sister or the hunter now. They were trapped there forever.

That part of the plan was done. It was now time to deal with The Council.

***

A bell tinkled at the bottom of the stairs in a small tenement building near the banks of the river. After a moment, a door on the top landing opened and a pair of feet in slippers began to shuffle slowly down the steps, leaving the door of the room ajar to reveal a little table surrounded by easels and brushes and cloths.

The room inside was sparsely furnished but nevertheless cluttered. A small bed in the dormer window, a dining chair at a table, and a soft lounge chair beside a cold, dark fireplace. The walls were covered in pictures, which were also stacked haphazardly on the floor and on every flat surface.

On the windowsill, above the end of the bed, in the rays of the morning sun, Mister Pluto was watching intently. His eyes were following a patch of nothingness, as black cats often do when they're deeply interested in something that doesn't exist.

Whatever the shape was, it had crept through the gap in the door that had been left open after the doorbell had rung, and appeared to be looking around. The formless entity moved silently around the confines of the tiny room, pausing frequently. It was examining the artwork, or at least that was the impression it gave.

Mister Pluto hadn't seen a ghost for a long time, and this one didn't seem to be doing much except looking at things, which was strange considering that it didn't have any eyes. He was thinking about springing on the apparition, but that would have meant moving, which he didn't feel very inclined to do. From past experience, pouncing on nothingness didn't achieve much anyway because you couldn't kill something that wasn't there.

He finally settled for tucking his head into his front paws and keeping watch with one open eye.

Whatever it was probably didn't care about cats.

Hardly anything did.

When the feet had got halfway down the stairs the bell tinkled again.

"Yes, yes!" shouted a voice, irritably. "Hold on. I'm coming."

The feet quickened their pace for two or three steps, before returning to their previous slow and methodical pattern.

A youth dressed in red and black was standing outside, clutching a small lumpy package wrapped in brown paper.

After some time, the door was opened by an old man. His shirt and trousers were covered in smudges of colour, and so were his hands.

"Jefferson... er... Squiggle, isn't it?" asked the youth, peering intently at the label of the package but finding himself unable to read the remainder of the name very well.

"Yes," replied the man.

The youth looked him up and down carefully with a critical expression, and gave the package an experimental squeeze, before handing it over carefully.

"More oils?" he asked.

"Oh yes. Thank you," replied the old man kindly, before closing the door gently and beginning his slow journey back up to the room at the top of the house.

This was good. He now had some browns and ochres, so he could finish that portrait of the lady with the funny lopsided smile he'd been working on for weeks.

The pictures he painted didn't sell particularly well, but he thought they were fairly good. He took some of them to exhibitions on occasions and sold a few, but mainly landscapes. That was what happened when you lived in a place that was heavily populated by Aylas. They liked their landscapes, which probably reminded them of the worlds they drew, he thought, but these were pictures of the real world, not their imaginary ones made up of funny symbols.

He didn't go to the exhibitions often. It was hard to carry paintings on foot, and the local gallery only had viewings that suited his kind of work every month or two. It didn't matter, he just enjoyed drawing and painting and creating, and he didn't spend money on much else, so it was a hobby he could afford. His part time job paid the living expenses, and any sales of artwork were a bonus.

Just before he turned the final corner at the top of the stairs, the shape slipped out of the partly open door to the room and hid itself in the confusion of light and shade in the stair railings along the top of the hallway.

It was on a mission. It had suspicions. There were things it had needed to know about the old man, and paying him a visit had been the best way it could think of to satisfy its curiosity.

There hadn't been much time, but it had seen enough.

***

When you discover where your enemy have made their camp, one of the most effective ways to weaken their morale is to wait until everyone is looking forward to dinner, and then bomb the kitchen.

The old man shuffled his way across the stone floor, sweeping imaginary dirt into a dustpan on a stick. There wasn't really any dirt, but sweeping was part of his job, so he swept, whether there was anything to sweep or not.

He had finished putting the cups and saucers out on the table. The water in the urn was boiling, the cakes were on their plates ready to serve, and the floor downstairs was clean, so there were a few minutes left to toddle round the upstairs gallery with the brush before the ladies arrived.

As he passed by an alcove between two pillars, he heard a noise.

"Pssst!"

That startled him. No-one else should be in the building yet. He put his brush into the slot on the dustpan, gathered the ends of the handles together at the top, and leaned them carefully against the wall.

"Yes! You! Jefferson, isn't it?"

He looked around but couldn't see anyone.

Then a shape moved in the shadows.

"Oh! You did give me a fright Ma'am!" he chuckled, patting himself on the chest with one hand.

"Sorry," she whispered. "Come a bit nearer."

Unaccustomed, as he was, to being propositioned by young girls on dark balconies, he took a moment to consider his options carefully. He didn't seem to have any. After all, she was an Ayla, so there was nothing to worry about, he was sure about that.

"I don't want to risk being seen!" she whispered by way of explanation.

"Oh yes Ma'am. Of course, Ma'am. Er... what can I do for you?"

She looked him up and down, which made him slightly more nervous.

"Would you like..." she said softly, "...a job?"

"But I already have a job Ma'am," he replied, after a moment's thought.

"Yes. But I mean a *proper* job."

"I don't understand Ma'am."

"You paint. You're an artist," she said. "It's very good work!"

He nodded. "Oh, thank you Ma'am."

"They don't treat you very well here, do they? I've got something you can do that's much more exciting," she said, giving him a smile and offering her hand.

The old man swallowed rather awkwardly.

"Come nearer to me," she whispered. "Where it's a bit darker."

18 - Jefferson's Project

As far as places to live were concerned, Jackie's home in the city was a typical urban apartment. Finding it had been relatively easy. It had a bedroom, bathroom, kitchen diner, blinds on the windows, and a big lock on the door. You could have imagined any professional or semi-professional office worker might live there if it wasn't for the bare wooden floors and stark grey walls covered in street art.

Jennifer had heard of the term 'Bohemian', meaning socially unconventional, and had appreciated that her sister might well indulge in a somewhat unorthodox and avant-garde lifestyle, so it hadn't been a surprise to discover that her tastes in furnishings might also be bordering on eccentric.

She hadn't expected to find a concrete table and chairs in the kitchen.

Nothing much had changed in the two weeks since she'd offered to let the old man move in, and it hadn't seemed a good idea to mention anything about her sister. It had been best to let him think the flat belonged to her.

At first, he'd not been sure it was right for him, but he was getting used to it, and she has been dropping in on him whenever she could find the time.

She appeared from around the corner with two mugs of tea, just as Jefferson was standing back to view the big patch of wall he had been working on.

"How's it going then?" she asked, putting the mugs down on the table with a gritty crunch. "Here's some tea!"

"Oh, thank you Ma... er Miss," he replied hesitantly.

It was taking him some time to get the hang of everything. Once he had been happy with the idea, she'd taken him back to his attic room to get a few home comforts, and Mister

Pluto, who was curled up on the windowsill, purring in the sunshine.

"It's a strange place for me here," he said, "and it's very odd art, but I'm getting used to it now".

"The art is looking good," replied Jennifer enthusiastically, gently caressing the odd spot of colour.

He gave her a meaningful stare over the top of his glasses.

"Really?" he said with an air of disbelief. "It all still looks like a mess to me."

"Well. Some of it is. But it's getting better thanks to you."

"I'm trying hard not to do too much to it at a time, like you said, but it's not easy when it needs such a lot of work."

"I know, but just take it slowly, give everything a chance to adjust to the changes each time, and it will all turn out right in the end," said Jennifer, reassuringly.

"This one's a whopper, isn't it?" he said, waving his hand at a patch of wall. It was all one mass of symbols and drawings.

"Yes! But look! Some colours are beginning to form already in various places. Just leave that one now, and let it develop while you work on something else."

"Yes Miss," said Jefferson, cheekily. "And all the wind?"

Jennifer scratched her chin thoughtfully.

"Wind is good at this stage, especially when it's such a big world. You can rub some of it out later, but right now it'll help to blow all the life around and mix it up."

"Right you are Miss. Wind is good! Got it."

"You have a very, *different*, taste in furniture and decor," he continued, choosing his words carefully.

Jennifer ran a few trains of thought through her mind.

Some of them crashed.

The real owner wouldn't be needing it again.

"We can change it if you want," she said.

"Oh really? There's no need Miss."

"That's alright Jefferson," she said, "I probably won't want to move back here, so you can change the place if you like. The important thing is that you're happy, and the work is taken care of."

"Oh, I'll do my best Miss."

"I know you will. But tell me, how is the new project that we discussed coming along?"

"Oh!" replied Jefferson enthusiastically, moving across to the opposite wall where he had set up an easel with a large canvas on it, covered by a cloth.

"I've made a start. Would you like to see it?"

"Yes, I would, very much so."

The old man removed the cloth, revealing a street scene consisting of an old stone building on the banks of a river, with a little bridge, and street lamps twinkling off the ripples in the water.

"Oh, that's very good Jefferson," said Jennifer, stroking some of the scene with her finger as she examined it closely. "You've got the storm gratings along the front really well, and the name on the sign. I expect details like that are hard to draw."

"Mind the wet paint though," cautioned the old man.

"It's alright," replied Jennifer. "It almost comes to life doesn't it."

"I've done better," he replied. "I'm not really used to city scenes."

"But you can see the inside very clearly through the windows," she said, peering closely at the details. "It doesn't have to be perfect."

"It's what you asked for," he replied. "Although I don't really understand why you want it."

"I thought it would be nice for you to have a memory of the place you've worked at for so long," she lied.

"Well, I'm enjoying this new adventure."

"That's good," said Jennifer.

"I really don't want to go back to my old job."

"When is the next meeting?" she asked. "Tuesday again I expect."

"That's right."

"That sounds like a good time to hand in your resignation then."

"Oh, do you think so?"

"Well, I think we ought to play a little trick on them as well. Don't you?" Jennifer considered the picture again, as her fingers moved over the damp brushstrokes. "I think it will be ready by then."

"What else do you want me to do to it?" he asked.

"Nothing. I think it's absolutely fine the way it is. Just put it away somewhere safe. I'll meet you here on Tuesday evening and we can go through the plan together."

"Right," said the old man. "That works for me."

"That's a deal then," replied Jennifer, closing her eyes.

"And… are you coming to the meeting as well this time?"

Jennifer opened one eye and looked at him as her outline began to fade.

"Oh yes," she said, mischievously, before she disappeared. "I'll be showing my face, don't you worry."

9

Day 21?

I have lost track of the days here in this strange place now, but it feels like it's about three weeks since I arrived. There is nothing to mark one week from another. Life is simply a succession of days.

We have settled into some form of routine here. The other girls were saying it's easier to manage with four people sharing the work, even though there is an extra mouth to feed. I seem to have taken on the task of cleaning out and re-laying the fire every day, so it's ready to light in the evening for cooking and warmth. That's fine as long as it doesn't rain, and then we're stuck indoors, or if the rain is only light we go into the wooden tower while the food cooks because it's nearer to the fire pit than the house.

Sometimes we'll all lay around the fire until it gets late, and the others will talk. I just pretend to be asleep, and listen.
Sam goes off hunting with his bow and arrow most nights and comes back with food, and he seems to like both the girls, so they share him.
Carrie doesn't seem very happy about that.

I don't think that was her idea.

They all share one bedroom. There's another, smaller room upstairs which was full of junk, but I cleared it up a bit and I live in there now.

The window opens above the roof of a woodshed at the back of the house, so I can climb down the drainpipe and come back to this room under the railway embankment to get some time away from them. They don't miss me, especially if they think I'm upstairs asleep.

I go out most nights exploring, and trying to make some sense of the various paths between worlds. A lot of that involves following Sam. He seems to know he can move between worlds, but doesn't understand it properly.

Despite many excursions, I've been unable to find an edge to this mess. It seems totally self-contained and it's not like any other existence I've ever seen.

It doesn't seem to consist of a collection of distinctly different worlds. It's more complicated than that, and much more fragmented. Some worlds look very similar to each other — too similar to be different ones.

More work is needed.

10

I've totally given up trying to put the day numbers on pages. I have no idea how long I've been here, and I'm only going to continue writing notes every few weeks anyway.

I've been away travelling every night when they think I'm asleep in my bed, making a map in an attempt to navigate my way through these twisted lands. The room under the arch is too damp and the walls are too gritty to do any sensible drawings on, so I'm using the walls in my room at the house.

It's a strange place with a lot of character. All the walls are peeling paint, which reveals the layers underneath. It looks like people have loved it for hundreds of years. There are pinks and browns and dark reds that have been overpainted with ochres and greys and yellows. It looks like one of my sister's drawings. I'm beginning to develop an appreciation of that kind of art now.

What's the world coming to?

The others seem to have set up a good home here, and for some reason I can't help feeling that the little house is happy to be loved again.

I get the impression that it was abandoned for a long time before they arrived here.
I didn't know that buildings could be alive.

I wasn't sure what the others expected when I turned up, and it was awkward not speaking to them. At some time they'd written their names on the wall near the front door, so I wrote mine at the bottom. I still don't really want them to know much about me, so I just wrote 'Ayla'. They don't seem to know what it means, but I'm okay with them calling me Ayla.

They all seem nice enough, but I have no intention of talking to them anyway.

11

From what I can piece together, the blonde girl, Tilly, got lost one day on the way back from school many years ago, and wasn't able to find her way home because the surroundings had changed. Familiar landmarks such as a wooden gate, a bridge and a railway station all seemed to have disappeared and her home didn't exist anymore.

She finished up discovering this abandoned house where she managed to make herself a new life. That's just typical of a normal world — you occasionally cross boundaries from time-to-time, so there may not have been anything especially odd about this world when she was younger.

Sam and Carrie arrived many years later, seemingly as a couple. They must have strayed off from the settlements on the plain and got lost too. Unless he knew of this place and brought her here on purpose. This also fits in with the normal structure of a single world that's developed into many paths. It's likely that the world Jennifer brought Carrie to was the same one that Tilly already lived in. They just stayed out on the plains where Tilly never went.

Whatever has happened to mix this world up with lots of others must have occurred fairly recently. I'm still working on understanding that. It's something to do with what I did in the cave.

There seems to be a sense of community, so a strange little girl who's willing to contribute to the chores is obviously a good thing. I knew it was a good idea not to go back to being an adult. At least I'm no threat to them, and their love triangle.

It's like a gathering of lost souls here, a kind of family. I'm beginning to like it, but I still don't feel as if this is where I'm meant to be.

I have continued to travel across boundaries and between worlds almost every night, and I'm beginning to understand what is happening here.

The new worlds I've drawn over the top of an existing established one seem to have created two types of discontinuity.

One of them is a boundary which takes you to an alternative reality that has split off from the same world as a result of following a different path when there has been a significant choice to make.

The other is a kind of crack where you can seemingly just walk between different worlds. This is definitely not normal.

Only Aylas travel between completely different worlds, and we have to think about it and know where we're going.

Different worlds aren't usually something that anyone can just walk between without realising it.

So, as a result of mixing up different worlds we have two distinct mechanisms at work here:

1. Boundaries that take you to another time in the same world, which is really another thread or branch. They feel kinda spongy to walk through. Usually, the place where you finish up is very similar to the one you were in, perhaps even so similar that you don't notice.

2. Cracks that take you to another different world. They're very sharp and it's difficult to know you've gone through them unless your mind is attuned to it.

We're not used to thinking about discontinuities as being anything other than the boundary type, paths between different times and places in the same world.

I'm still spending my time between the house and the room under the arch. The sense of belonging to a kind of family is somehow addictive, I've not felt that way for a very long time, but I also need my space to get away from them now and again.

13

Sam appears to be noticing that this world doesn't work properly.

This is probably because it doesn't.

He knows about travelling through boundaries. He just doesn't understand how the ones here work. On reflection, why would he? I'm only beginning to understand them because I know how this world, or set of worlds, was created.

Whenever he goes off travelling, I have to tag along out of sight and make sure he gets back. He knows about moving between different worlds, like an Ayla, but that doesn't always work here because some of the places he wants to go don't exist, and I still don't understand how he is a destroyer-of-worlds.

I'm going to have to keep a very close eye on him, otherwise he'll get lost and then no-one will have any food, and I'll also have no way to kill him. I somehow get the impression that Tilly used to hunt for food when she was here alone for years, but finding food for one is very different than finding it for four.

Their life as they know it now would end if Sam disappeared. I don't want that to happen. There must be a way to solve that problem.

14

It's interesting to listen to them all talking.
The fire pit still seems to be the main gathering
place.

Sam was trying to explain to them about dreams,
and how they allow people to connect with the
other copies of themselves that exist in other
threads of the world. Tilly understood that. I
didn't know that, because I'm not human and it's
apparent that my dreams are not like theirs.

It means he's some sort of hybrid. He understands
things in the same way that humans do, and he
seems to know he isn't one, but he doesn't know
what he really is or where he came from.

He has memories that extend some way back in
time, but not right back to childhood. That doesn't
appear to bother him. He struggles with it
sometimes but dismisses it.

Sometimes, when Sam comes home after hunting
and I'm asleep in my room in the house, I seem to
share his thoughts in the form of a dream. He's
very confused. He doesn't know what he is, or what
he wants. He doesn't realise he's supposed to be a
destroyer-of-worlds.

He believes his purpose in life is to make things better and he seems to be hunting for something, but he doesn't know what it is.

He likes Carrie, because she's kinda strong and more dominant, but she has a very closed mind. Tilly is more fun and easy-going, and he can't make his mind up which one he likes the best between the two of them.

I dunno what he thinks about me at all. I know I'm supposed to get rid of him, and I could easily get him lost somewhere, but that wouldn't solve the problem, it would only put an end to what everyone has built here, and he would still be out there causing problems somewhere else.

These worlds wanted Carrie to survive.
I suppose I'm their creator, so I ought to be trying to understand what they want and do the right thing.

I'm beginning to sound like my sister, that's the sort of thing she would say.

I need him to teach one of the others how to hunt before I kill him, otherwise none of us will have any food.

15

As tertiary creatures you'd expect Sam and I to share some common traits.

I do seem to be able to tell what he's thinking sometimes, and if we are all asleep together in the house I often dream about what he did during the day. It's weird — in the sense of suggesting something supernatural or unearthly.

Well, that's what the others would call us anyway. We're certainly unearthly as far as they would be concerned.
If they knew us that well.

If there is some link between us that allows me to share his dreams then maybe there's a way for me to influence his thoughts as well.

I don't understand why that might be. I did create him, but you don't have any control over the things you create. There's no reason why we should be connected in that way, or why I should be able to make him do what I want.

I wonder what the stars are that twinkle in the sky.

Tilly and Carrie think they are all suns, with other worlds around them that people might live on. I didn't draw them and there is no symbol for them. They just seem to appear uninvited above every world. Tilly seems to think they're so far away that no-one can ever go fast enough to get to them.

Our daddy went to the stars, a long time ago. He thought he could go fast enough to reach them. I wonder if he's got there yet, or whether he ever will.

If they are other worlds, it should have been possible for either my sister or I to get to them much easier than he could, and we could have taken him with us, but that would have meant knowing exactly what they looked like, which we'd only have known if we'd already been there. We couldn't help him. That's why he had to go the slow way and travel through all the distance between them to get there.

If the stars are the same in every world he might be up there somewhere in my sky. Perhaps he still thinks of us and wonders what we're doing.

16

Today I made more progress. I pretty much know my way around this universe now. That's what it is, an isolated collection of worlds with a boundary, and no contact with the outside. That's a universe.

I went out to the area where Tilly had originally got lost, and found where the iron bridge was. It would go over a little stream that joins the river, if it existed in this world.

It does exist in some worlds, and so does the wooden gate and the railway station. Some worlds have both a gate and a station. Others only have a gate. Most of the ones that have a school also have the iron bridge, probably because it was put there when the school was built. Some worlds, like the one we're in now, don't have any of those things. They're either the same world at a different point in time, or they're copies of this world where events proceeded in alternative ways because different decisions were made.

That's exactly why Tilly got lost on her way home from school. She just walked through some boundaries into another time in the same world.

When Aylas travel, we think about where we want to be, and we disappear. For a moment we're nowhere, or everywhere, it depends how you look at it, and then we re-emerge in the time and place we thought about, which is almost always in another world. The cracks here don't work like that. Anyone can just walk into them and suddenly, without any warning, they're somewhere else. What I don't understand is why going back the same way, through the same cracks, doesn't always take people back where they'd originally come from. They should do, so that's what I need to understand next.

I have tried drawing collections of symbols to create new worlds, but they remain just that. Collections of symbols. No sign of life appears to develop in them, not even the tiniest tinge.
It was both an experiment to check whether this universe worked like a normal one, but also a way to build myself somewhere to escape into if I ever needed to get away from here.
The fact that it doesn't work means there is something distinctly different here. Perhaps it's too small? Perhaps being a totally isolated universe makes it non-expandable?

I can't think of a way to test either of those assertions from inside it.

17

The odd-looking white wooden building in the clearing is some kind of Signal Tower. I found lamps and flags and other things in various cupboards and drawers that would have been used to send messages.

There's a rackety old ladder going all the way up the centre to a room at the top with windows that look out across the world in all directions. Some of the rungs are rotten or missing, but it holds my weight. I don't think the others have ever been up there. If they have, they've never talked about it while I've been with them.

It was obviously built for some specific purpose, but that's unclear because there's nothing as far as the eye can see that it could have communicated with.

Tilly has discovered that Sam can travel to other worlds. She thinks he might be able to take her home after all these years. He doesn't think he can, and I don't either. She wants him to take her with him when he goes off hunting, but he's reluctant to do that.

I still seem to connect with Sam when I am asleep. It's unnerving sometimes, so I sleep in my room under the archway at night more often these days, where I'm not near enough to him for our minds to connect.

I need him to teach one of the others how to hunt with the bow-and-arrow before I kill him, so I'm trying to make him think he needs a companion when he goes off on adventures. I suspect it may work if I fall asleep and dream about it because he might also share my dreams as well as the other way round.

I'm still no further with my understanding of how he's a destroyer-of-worlds, or what I'm supposed to do to get rid of him.

He still can't make up his mind whether he's happier with Carrie or Tilly and he is getting more and more uptight about that as every day goes by.

~~ 18 ~~

My plotting and dreaming seems to have worked.
Sam has started teaching Tilly to hunt. She has
her own bow and arrows now, and he is taking
her off with him on adventures to other worlds.
Carrie doesn't seem to care, but I can tell that she
does really. I follow them on most trips to see where
they go, but don't stay with them all the time. It's a
good chance to explore, and improve the details on
my maps.

Tilly seems to find it exciting, and I think she's
starting to learn how to travel between worlds.
Sometimes, when she is talking about places and
has vivid memories of them, I can see her aura
flicker, and she doesn't look so solid.
I don't know what to make of that. I didn't know it
was a transferable skill.
One day she'll manage to do it without him.
I just hope she knows that she can. That's a bit
scary.
I'll have to keep a lookout for that happening, in
case she has problems getting back.

These days I find myself sitting on the riverbank more often, watching the ripples spread out across the water, or simply looking at the clouds.

There's something relaxing about these worlds, even though they are a jumbled-up mess. Or perhaps it's sharing all my dreams with Sam.

I never wanted to be part of a family, but being a member of a closely-knit group is rewarding. Each of us has responsibilities and things to do, and life works. I always thought that having responsibilities would be a very restrictive way to live, but it's not.

When people do the things they're good at it makes life better and easier for everyone, and you get to learn from others.

I'll be sad when it ends.

19

Sam is sleeping with Tilly more often now and ignoring Carrie. That doesn't make her pleased. Last night, when we returned, Sam had brought back another gun with him. A Beretta, like the other one he has in his bag which no-one else knows about except me. I've never seen him use anything except a bow and arrow. I'm sure he has some kind of plan, although I can't imagine what would involve the use of two guns.

Carrie was not impressed when she found it. She does have a habit of going off into depressive rants when she gets upset, and she doesn't like the idea of him keeping things from her. That's one of the reasons he likes Tilly, because she is more intellectual and doesn't get snippy about things.

Carrie is upset that he's taken Tilly under his wing and is paying a lot more attention to her these days.

I continue working on my maps and it's starting to make sense at last but it's worrying.

We know some discontinuities are simple boundaries between different times and places in the same world, but others are cracks.

It's as if all the different worlds that exist here are stacked on top of each other like sheets of glass, and they all have cracks in them.

If the sheet of glass above or below you has a crack that crosses the one in your world, you can find yourself jumping up or down across the layers, and finish up in a completely different world to the one you started from.

That's the difference between the types of discontinuity.

Normally, a set of similar worlds that differ only by the events that have occurred in them are happy to sit on top of each other comfortably.

Mixing many unrelated worlds together creates a stack of existences that are all very different, and don't sit together well. They're different sizes and the surfaces are different textures, so they grate together and aren't very stable.

If you stack enough of them up they'll fall over, unless something is pinning them together.

20

The thing that locks all these different worlds together here is that white wooden Signal Tower.

A few worlds have no house in the clearing, some have no school, or no wooden gate, or no iron bridge, or the river runs a different course, or the clumps of trees and paths are different, but every world I've been to has a clearing in the forest with a Signal Tower.
If you make a mark on the side of it, you'll find it on every tower.
It's the same building that exists in every world.

I don't understand why it's here, unless perhaps the tower was part of the original world on the cave wall along with all the life that's also here.

Maybe the ones I drew have somehow swirled around it and the life in the original world has got all mixed up with them.

Sam is getting more and more depressed from day to day.

He wants to be with Carrie because he somehow thinks she is his future, but he isn't happy because he also wants to be with Tilly, and she likes him too.
When I close my eyes, I can feel that.
For some reason, perhaps because I'm trying to share my dreams with him, it feels like he is growing closer to me and distancing himself from the other two girls.

That's scary. I mean, I wanted to share my dreams with Sam, as a way of trying to make him do what I wanted, but I didn't think it would have that effect.

21

Okay, so this is bad.

More cracks are appearing throughout this stack of worlds at an increasing rate. Every time I go out, I find more of them, and I can't keep my maps up to date any longer.

It looks like when something goes through a crack it stresses it, and that can cause it to spread and grow longer. That's why going in the reverse direction through the same fault doesn't always take you back to where you came from.
The more cracks there are, the more people walk through them and that creates new ones, and makes the existing ones worse.

The situation on the plain has gradually worsened over the ages as a result of all the settlers moving around in groups, but something has protected this strip of forest, probably the river on one side that no-one crosses, and the railway embankment on the other side where few settlers venture under the arch. I've started climbing over the embankment now when I want to be on the other side. I don't like the feel of going through that archway, there's a gap in the middle of it that doesn't seem to exist in any world.

A few small cracks don't make much difference to the strength of something, but when they begin to grow longer and join together it's a different story. The structural integrity of a world gets a lot weaker, and the cracks start spreading faster. With these worlds all stacked on top of each other it's even worse because they spread outwards but also upwards and downwards into other layers.

This universe is living on borrowed time.

I climbed up the Signal Tower again last night. From there you can see the entire circle of the sky, all the way from the hills at the back, to what looks like the sea way off in the distance across the tops of the forest over the other side of the river. This stack of worlds is held together like a pile of papers stuck on a nail. That's why exactly the same structure exists in every world. There are lots of worlds, but only one Signal Tower.

Until I can work out a solution to the problem, everyone will need to be very careful. At some point, when it gets weak enough, the whole structure is going to collapse. The entire stack of worlds will shatter into thousands of fragments, and everything will fly apart with a great big bang.

22

I've been thinking again. This world has gone downhill rapidly, and it began soon after I arrived here.

Before I came along these people were enjoying a relatively happy life, and then I turned up and started following them about. One person going out hunting very stealthily didn't do much damage, but when you squeeze two excited people through a crack, or even follow behind someone, it starts off a cascade.

I started going through all the worlds trying to map the discontinuities, which made cracks bigger and weaker. Since I encouraged Sam to take Tilly with him and I've had to tag along behind as a threesome, it's made the situation even worse.

My arrival has also had an impact on Sam. He was once with Carrie and was relatively happy. Then, when he found Tilly, he was divided, but they rubbed along as a threesome. Connecting with me, and my dreams, has had some deep effect on him that I don't understand.

He doesn't seem happy with either of them now, and he doesn't know why, but everyone's life was okay until I turned up and now their existence is under threat, and nobody is happy.

The conclusion is obvious.

The destroyer-of-worlds is not the bow-and-arrow man.

The destroyer-of-worlds is me.

~~ 24 ~~

This is the final straw.

It came to a climax last night because I had to go out looking for both the girls, and Sam, who had all gone off in different directions and got lost. I managed to run around after them leaving enough hints to enable them to find their way home, but it took me two whole days to get Carrie back, and even then I was only able to get her very close to the right time and place.

Fortunately, she is ok.

What happened last night will have caused hundreds more cracks in dozens of worlds and, just like some relationships, they never heal.

Perhaps Sam also senses what I sense now, which is that the end of civilisation is approaching rapidly. This collection of worlds is now so badly damaged that I imagine its life is measured in hours.

We can't go on like this and it's probably already too late. Venturing any distance from the clearing is like walking on breaking ice. I'm reluctant to go anywhere now in the darkness.

It's difficult enough spotting changes in the surroundings in daylight, never mind when you can't see anything much around you, and if you do find yourself somewhere else there's no guarantee you'll be able to find your way back, or even if the place you came from still exists.

The impression is that everything is closing in on us, although in reality it's all getting bigger.

There's nothing more I can do now.

We survived the night, but I didn't sleep.

I don't know what will come of us all when the universe shatters.

Alternative realities are being created all the time when a range of possibilities can happen. We think we have chosen one of them, but they all still exist.

Perhaps there will be remaining fragments that are large enough to live in. Maybe some fragments containing copies of Tilly and Carrie might have a future now that Tilly can hunt better.

I have no idea what will happen to tertiary creatures like Sam and me. We are only able to exist in one world at a time, but in alternative realities of the same world there may be copies of us that survive in different circumstances. We've both had options to choose different paths. Perhaps there'll be one where we're together. Somehow the idea of that feels nice.

Maybe when it ends with a big bang everyone gets what they deserve, or Destiny offers them a choice.

I didn't specifically draw a symbol for her in this universe, but maybe there only needs to be one.

Your Destiny is supposed to be where you finish up, but I have a feeling it might also be a waypoint where you have a chance to start again.

Perhaps you get a shot at more than one of them.

At the end of the world maybe we all just, philosophically speaking, choose a fragment that we like and cling on. Who knows, but we're about to find out.

I never wanted to have a big adventure like this, but it looks like I'm now going on another one. Perhaps what I've discovered will be useful to someone. I will leave this journal on the window sill in my room before I say goodbye to the little house.

I have a feeling it will look after it for me.

– JM

20 - The Resignation

Jennifer wriggled, trying to find a comfortable position where the edge of the stone chair didn't chafe the back of her legs.

"Do you actually like these, Jefferson?" she asked, tapping the seat with her hand.

The old man wrinkled his brow. He didn't really like them at all, they always scuffed the back of his trouser legs. They were the most impractical and uncomfortable things he'd ever sat on. Even Mister Pluto wouldn't sit on them.

"Well..." he began.

"That means no," interrupted Jennifer. "There's no need to worry about speaking the truth."

The old man nodded sagely.

"I thought they might involve some special memories, that's all."

"Not really. I'll think of a way to get rid of them," she said. "We can easily find something better and more comfortable to sit on."

Jefferson thought about that for a moment. Almost anything would be better, even the boxes he'd used to bring things from his old room.

"I've put some final touches on the painting," he said, rising awkwardly from the gritty seat and making his way towards the easel. "I know you said it was fine, but it seemed to need a few more details."

Jennifer watched as he lifted the work off the stand and removed the cloth.

"Oh yes!" she exclaimed, squinting at the patches of fresh colour that popped out at her from various places. "Very nice attention to detail indeed. I like the sign on the tavern. It really does look as if it's lit."

"Thank you Miss," he replied, bringing it a bit closer. "The paint is still not fully dry, so take care."

Jennifer stroked her finger very gently over the sign, being careful not to touch it too hard and cause a smudge. The old man was sure that, for a moment, he saw it flicker.

"Oh!" she exclaimed. "You've called it a Hotel on the sign. I thought it was an Inn."

The old man nodded.

"Yes. I didn't think you'd mind," he said, nervously. "It just tripped off the tongue better. **The Hotel Kafalonia**. It has a kind of ring to it."

"That's fine," replied Jennifer, kindly. "There's nothing wrong with a bit of artistic licence."

She considered the total picture. It did look very real.

"There's one very important thing missing though," she said, sternly.

"Oh! What's that?" asked Jefferson, sounding a little nervous.

"You haven't put your... er... signature on it," she said, struggling for the appropriate words. "Everyone should put their mark on their creations."

The old man's face burst into a smile.

"Well, if you think it's that good and it's finished, we can soon remedy that," he said.

From the drawer of a nearby cabinet he produced a fine brush and a pot of red ink.

"I always sign my works in red," he explained, as he unscrewed the cap of the bottle with a degree of ceremony and drew his squiggle in the bottom corner with a practised flourish.

The work was placed reverently back on the easel, and Jennifer went across to have another look at it.

It really was a masterpiece, she thought. The stone bridge over the river, with the lamp posts. The dark, imposing sky, with streaks of grey clouds drifting across the full moon, reflected in the ripples of the water. The large stone hall with its vaulted roof occupied prime position in the scene, with the red and white sign over the tavern door casting a shadow on the partly-open awning. She touched the front of the building gently, and the light from the chandelier flickered almost imperceptibly in the windows, making faint yellow patches on the damp road below. The signature of the creator in the corner made the illusion unique.

"I'm glad you like it," said the old man.

"I love it," replied Jennifer. "It's perfect."

"Thank you very much. I try to do the best I can."

"We all do, Jefferson," observed Jennifer, before suddenly realising the time. "You need to go now, or you'll be late for the meeting, and that will never do. Being late on your last day!"

"Oh yes Miss. I'm rather looking forward to it," he said. "And you're definitely planning to be there, so we can play our little trick on them?"

"Of course, that's what we agreed. You go ahead and get everything setup, as usual, and I'll be along shortly."

***

In the stone hall with its vaulted roof, the yellow glow from the chandelier fell once again on the circular table, stacked with its usual assortment of cakes and teapots. Amidst the muttering of chatter and the tinkling of spoons, Number One cleared her throat before turning her head towards the old man who was stood beside the table with his cloth over his arm.

"Firstly, I note with relief that our manservant has returned at last," she said, in her best dismissive voice. "I trust you had a good... holiday."

"Oh! Thank you, Ma'am. I did indeed," he replied nonchalantly.

"And perhaps next time you would care to tell us in advance," grumbled Number Three. "We've been having to fetch our own tea and cakes."

"Yes, it's not right," grumbled Number Four, dislodging an errant crumb from her lips with a wrinkled finger. "We have important work to do."

Jefferson smiled.

"I apologise Ma'am," he muttered, and then, attempting to conceal the tiniest of smirks, he added carefully, "I assure you it will not happen again."

"And I've had to make excuses for you too," said Number One sternly, turning her gaze to the right, and fixing her deputy with the stare-of-death. "Where have you been while this creature was threatening our existence?"

"Yeah, sorry!" said Number Six rather awkwardly. "I've been rather busy with important matters of my own."

"Well, don't let that happen again either," scolded Number One. "I really do need to know where you are." Number Six looked up at her from behind her masque, as a puppy might look up to its mummy. "Anyway," continued Number One, "let's have the first item of the evening's business, which I believe is concerned with the status of the destroyer-of-worlds."

Number Six handed her a single sheet of paper, which she examined carefully.

"Oh!" she said after a brief moment. "This report would suggest that the agent we appointed, Jennifer Marlow, has been successful. It appears that the creature's desires have been satisfied. Whatever that means."

"It means the creature has not necessarily been destroyed, but is no longer a threat," replied Number Six. "I can explain, if you like?"

Number One nodded without looking up from the report sheet. The attempts to kill her deputy had failed, but now she had returned this would definitely be her last night.

"Well, it's like this," began Number Six, pushing her chair backwards with a screech, and rising to address the others. "Let's just say that I know Jennifer Marlow very well, and I've been taking a very close interest in all the proceedings of the last few weeks."

"Your recommendation was a good one," conceded Number One with barely disguised hatred in her voice.

Number Six nodded in a gesture of appreciation.

There was a general muttering from the assembled members.

"*You* put her forward?" exclaimed Number Three.

"Indeed, she did," continued Number One. "Although I was not initially convinced, it appears that she was the perfect choice to solve the problem."

"Thank you," said Number Six. "It's true that the creature was a hunter, brought into existence by the drawing of one specific tertiary symbol – the bow-and-arrow of course - but it was targeted very specifically to hunt one particular person, and would do whatever was necessary to capture them."

The committee mumbled while Number Six drew another breath.

"This is one reason why it gained the reputation of being a destroyer of worlds," she continued. "It is a somewhat unfortunate perception of its true nature, however it could be considered strangely accurate in many ways."

The assembled members considered this carefully, to the accompaniment of a rattling of saucers and the tinkling of spoons.

"It is however gone now, and will find its true purpose with the eventual capture of the creature to which it was originally bound. But now, my time here is done too, and I must say goodbye."

"You're talking very strangely today Number Six," noted the leader, regarding her with a quizzical expression as if somehow coming to the realisation that all was not quite as it seemed.

"I'm sorry," she said, in a voice which could easily have sounded like the kind of apology someone would make when they had been left with no choice, and were being forced into doing something terrible which they would subsequently regret, but probably not very much, and not for very long.

She motioned to the old man, who quickly backed away by taking several hasty steps towards the light switches on the wall near the door.

There was a click, and the lights went out.

"It's all gone dark," muttered Number Two, after a brief pause.

There was a clang.

"Oooo. I've dropped my spoon," squeaked the frustrated voice of Number Five.

"JEFFERSON!" called Number Four, angrily. "Turn the lights back on, you stupid man!"

There was no response.

"JEFFERSON! If this is some kind of joke, it's not funny. You just wait until I get my hands on you!" shouted Number Five.

The sound of chair legs scraping on the polished wooden floor echoed through the hall, followed by the crash of plates and teapots as someone tried to stand up but caught their knees under the table.

"Don't worry," grumbled Number One. "I'll see to it myself."

After a few moments of panic, the lights came on.

Four sets of eyes gazed across in the direction of the door, but Jefferson was nowhere to be seen, only Number One with her hand on the light switches.

"Where's that stupid old man gone?" cried Number Three, looking around furtively.

"And Number Six!" exclaimed another voice.

Number One strode through the doorway into the scullery, and returned almost immediately.

"They're not here," she said angrily as her frustration gave way to puzzlement. "Well, that's all very strange."

A slender hand reached out towards the remaining pink cake on one of the saucers that had not fallen off its stand.

"That's mine!" cried Number Three. "You know I like those."

***

"You can turn them back on now, Jefferson," called a voice from somewhere near the centre of the room. There was a faint click and the hall was illuminated once again by its pale-yellow chandelier, revealing Number Six, who had removed her masque, standing in the centre of an empty floor. Only a few crumbs remained, scattered in a circle around the spot where once had been six chairs and a table full of teapots and cake stands.

"Oh!" said the old man. "That was a good trick! I can see you've done *that* before."

"Thank you," replied Jennifer, walking slowly across towards him, rubbing her forehead where the masque had left a faint red mark. "Indeed I have. Too many times these last few weeks. I'm beginning to get the hang of it now."

"You could entertain people," mused Jefferson. "People would pay to see that!"

"Yes… maybe…" replied Jennifer, thoughtfully. It wasn't a career that she had considered, but if she ever got tired of creating worlds, she could think of worse things to do in her retirement. "Right now, we still have work to do."

"Oh yes. I suppose so. We'll need some new furniture for a start," he said.

"Yes, and we need some new people. But for now," she said, offering the old man her hand, "turn out the lights again please - and this time we'll go home."

21 - Alkira

Jennifer looked out through the vines across the valley while Alkira topped up her mug from the little teapot.

"I'm sorry I misled you," she said. "I didn't mean to."

"It's okay," replied Jennifer. "I know you didn't."

"The Council had asked three of my friends about you, and they wanted to talk to you, but none of them were able to contact you, for some reason."

Jennifer glanced awkwardly at the message frame on the wall.

"No... I... er... don't keep in touch with many people these days," she said sadly.

"So, I said I would have a go at calling you, but when you actually answered I really didn't know exactly what to say."

"I realised that," said Jennifer. "It was one of the first things that felt odd."

Alkira nodded.

"They told me why they wanted to see you and what it was all about, but I had to make a lot of it up as I went along," she confessed.

"It showed," said Jennifer, with a little wink at her friend. "I thought something wasn't right, and when the creature in the forest wasn't the way you described it to be, and you weren't here when I returned home I was even more suspicious."

"I really was going to come and look after your worlds though," said Alkira reassuringly. "But you were back much sooner than I thought."

"I needed to know more about the bow and arrow symbol..." began Jennifer.

"...so you found your father's book," interrupted Alkira.

"Yes..."

"...in the trunk that was with all your old toys."

Jennifer's expression turned to one of amazement.

"I packed them all up when your dad didn't return from his expedition to Pertinax," explained Alkira. "I wasn't sure exactly where they'd all got put away, but the book contains a lot of information that nobody really understands. You presumably found what you were looking for?"

"Yes, I did," confirmed Jennifer. "And it was very interesting indeed."

"I'm sure it was. Much more interesting than my impromptu ramblings about the tertiary symbols then."

"You did a pretty good job, you got most of the myths and legends right anyway."

Alkira nodded.

"That's good to know."

"And The Council are gone," continued Jennifer brightly, after a moment.

"So I hear," mused Alkira. "That's good. Just out of interest, what happened to them?"

"They're in a better place," answered Jennifer with a sigh. "They weren't bad people, they were just useless. It wasn't really fair to kill them all."

"No, probably not," agreed her friend. "It was their leader who caused all the trouble, you can't blame them all for that. What if they come back?"

Jennifer shook her head.

"They won't come back. I made a new friend you see, an old man called Jefferson. He's very good at painting, so we created a little world together. Just big enough for five old women, with plenty of bottomless teapots and a never-ending supply of pink cakes and mille feuille. He painted it, I helped bring it to life, and I transported them all there, along with their furniture and everything that made the place look familiar. None of them will even realise what's happened. It's like a hotel stocked with everything they'll ever need, open

24/7 for the rest of eternity," explained Jennifer. "They'll have to go and fetch their own tea and cakes from the kitchen though. Their manservant resigned rather unexpectedly," she added, with a cheeky grin.

"And you're sure they can't get out?" said Alkira, now sounding worried.

"Life will just repeat for them in a loop until they eventually die. Even if they manage to get an outside door open there's no world out there, it will just open onto a soft fog that they won't be able to walk far into. There's nowhere to go because I only brought the building to life, it has no surroundings." Alkira raised her eyebrows. "They can check out anytime they like," continued Jennifer. "But they can never leave."

"I see," said Alkira thoughtfully. "Good job then. And the bow-and-arrow creature?"

"Is neutralised, yes," replied Jennifer, pulling out the chair and sitting down at the table with her. "But we need to talk about that. It's complicated."

"I see," replied Alkira cautiously, who appeared to be taking all these new turns of events in her stride.

"I sent my sister off to confront him," said Jennifer.

"Jackie? I've not spoken to her for years. You two were always up to mischief as I remember."

Jennifer hugged her mug of tea thoughtfully.

"Yes, we were," she replied, the memories of childhood now flooding back once again. "We had lots of adventures together…"

"And killed lots of people!" interrupted Alkira with a cheeky grin.

"…and fixed lots of worlds," continued Jennifer," giving her the side-eye. "But you saw what happened after Dad went off exploring."

Alkira nodded. She remembered those days all too well. The girls had no real sense of family anymore after that, and no-one to keep them focused on any path.

"Jackie hated me ever since we broke up years ago," continued Jennifer, sadly.

"I know," replied Alkira, soothingly. "But I'm really pleased for you both. It sounds like you made up and managed to work as a team again."

"Yes, and no," replied Jennifer, cryptically. "I called her, but we never really made up." Alkira gazed thoughtfully at the wall. "She was only pretending. I still detected that bubbling hatred that she's always had for me. It was never going to go away."

"But she came when you called."

"Yes, I know. Rather too quickly, I thought. That was another thing that seemed odd. It was too good to be true that she would make up so easily."

"Oh, I see," said Alkira.

"Jackie was the one who had drawn all those proto-worlds on the walls of that cave, on top of a perfectly good world that was already there, put the symbol for the bow-and-arrow man in the middle of them, and then scuffed them all up into a mess. They were typical of her style, and they'd all been smudged about by one person about the same size and proportions as me..."

"...and after the council had exhausted their resources attempting to defeat it, she suggested to them that you might be able to help?" said Alkira.

"Exactly, but she never really thought I could. She just wanted to get rid of me as well. Even if I couldn't destroy it, her intention was to strand us both in the twisted world she'd created."

"…and then she would be able to make a move to take over The Council herself," added Alkira, nodding her head. She was always quick to pick up the plot.

"The symbol does create a bow-and-arrow man, and he is inextricably connected to the Ayla who draws it," explained Jennifer. "If you draw one, he'll hunt you down and take you, forever. You're not supposed to draw one and then run away. Well, not far anyway. The only way to satisfy him is to be caught. There's nowhere to hide. He'll kill anyone that gets in his way, and he'll destroy anything that stops him from getting to you. Creating him is a last resort. It's your way out of the world when you're fed up with the life you've got. Jackie had heard of the destroyer-of-worlds, and thought it sounded like the answer to her problems. So, she created one, but it isn't what she thought it was going to be."

"But won't he kill her?"

"That's where the legend is misunderstood," said Jennifer as Alkira sat forward to listen more intently.

"The book says that *when the symbol is drawn a destroyer-of-worlds is created.*"

Alkira thought about this until a sparkle of understanding appeared in her eyes.

"Oh!" she said after a moment. "So, the destroyer-of-worlds is not necessarily the bow-and-arrow man that the symbol produces?"

"I don't think so," replied Jennifer. "The Ayla who draws it becomes the destroyer-of-worlds."

Alkira thought about this all again, for what seemed a very long time.

"And the bow-and-arrow man goes hunting for the Ayla who drew him, and kills her because she has become the destroyer-of-worlds!" she said, her face lighting up as she realised the implications of the whole story.

"Er, well, yes, but not quite," said Jennifer. "The bow-and-arrow man it creates does come hunting for her, but the world she destroys is her own. I found the symbol in the same section of the book as Hope, Fate and Destiny, so the expression 'destroyer-of-worlds' is probably meant to have a philosophical meaning rather than a physical one."

"Why did she ever agree to go?" interrupted Alkira.

"She didn't want to," replied Jennifer. "I had to keep the truth from her. She'd never have gone if she'd known that the bow-and-arrow man was really hunting for her. I just told her what she needed to hear."

"So, you gave up your sister as bait to a hunter?"

"Bait isn't really the right word," replied Jennifer, now beginning to sound slightly irritated. "It's more like starting out on a new adventure. It was for the best."

"But if he was connected to both of you it wasn't a foregone conclusion. You could have surrendered yourself to him instead of giving him your sister," argued Alkira.

"I suppose I could, but I'm not ready for my world to be destroyed yet. I quite like my life the way it is. Jackie was different. She wasn't happy, she was never going to be a good creator of worlds and they all hated her. She needed a better life. It was a sacrifice I had to make."

"Sending her off to have her world destroyed? Is that really a better life?"

Jennifer looked up very slowly from her mug, straight into Alkira's big dark eyes, and the room seemed to go unusually quiet. Her friend was still missing the point. Did she really have to explain it in detail? Apparently so. She took a big breath, followed by an equally big sigh.

"Different civilisations have various names for him," she said very patiently. "But most of them use a similar symbol. There are few ways to call him up at will, most people have to wait, and search, and hope that they find a better life. You need to understand the purpose of bringing him into existence. That's why you need to read the book first. Not every mythical creature who wants to shoot you through the heart with a bow-and-arrow is trying to kill you."

The sounds of the outside world slowly filtered back into the little room as the two figures sat gazing into each other's eyes.

Alkira broke the silence.

"I see," she said quietly. "So, Jackie isn't dead then?"

"I hope not, but it will have been easier for her if she's taken my advice and gone back looking like an adult. I gave her a chance. That world is fractured enough already without making perceptions any more complicated than they have to be, but I have a feeling that a girl I rescued in the forest has some part to play. The world wanted me to save her."

Alkira nodded slowly and picked up Jennifer's hand.

"So, it was a kind thing to do then," she said. "At least you know how it works now, and you can always draw your own bow-and-arrow man one day when you get tired of this life and want a new adventure."

"Perhaps," replied Jennifer with a sigh. "I'm not sure about that. The one she created was connected to my mind as well as hers. The book says every Ayla can draw only one of them. If the universe can't tell us apart, maybe we only get one between us and Jackie has already drawn ours."

Alkira squeezed Jennifer's fingers.

"Well, you'll never know until the day comes that you want to try it."

"True," said Jennifer, brightening up a bit and snatching her hand away. "But that day is not today. I have work to do."

"That's very true. There'll be new organisational plans to make," said Alkira. "I have some candidates lined up for a new council, but we'll need a leader. I've already talked it over with the others, and we'd like that to be you."

Jennifer fell silent for a moment. Being the leader of a new order wasn't what she'd had in mind. Changes would need to be made, but it sounded like a challenge.

"Thank you. I'd like that," she said. "But there are a few loose ends I need to tidy up first, if you don't mind? To keep things from unravelling."

"Of course," replied her friend, kindly. "Take all the time you need."

At that moment, a faint rustling in the greenery across the opening of her room caused Jennifer to twist round. A small creature was sitting uncomfortably on the stalk of a vine, shuffling awkwardly from one foot to the other. Jennifer squinted at its silhouette against the bright background. The thin dumpy little body with matchstick stalks for legs, the tail which bobbed up and down as it maintained its balance on the vine, and the pointy beak, left her in no doubt as to what it was, even if it did appear to have a scrawny neck which was disproportionally long for the rest of its body and head.

"Oh, look Alkira, it's a bird!" squeaked Jennifer. "I've never seen one here! I've always wanted some, but nobody knows who owns this world or where the drawing of it is!" she cried.

Jennifer was fond of watching birds whenever she was away visiting other worlds. They were either small, cute bundles of energy that bounced around between twigs, or large graceful creatures that soared high in the skies. This one looked like something that had been boil-washed and then inexpertly dried with a blowtorch. It needed the benefit of a couple of thousand years of evolution before it could be said to fall into either of those categories, but it was definitely a winged creature of some sort.

The proto-bird fixed its gaze on Alkira with a very puzzled expression, as if it had suddenly remembered something that it wasn't aware it had ever known, and made an excited attempt to sing with joy, which Jennifer thought sounded like someone trying to free-up a rusty hinge.

From the other side of the table, Alkira looked past the back of Jennifer's head, across into its little black eyes, and gave it an almost imperceptible nod.

It wasn't every day that a little creature actually got to meet its maker.

22 - Blossom

A gentle breeze blew pink blossom off the trees near the church. It drifted through the black iron railings and gathered near the feet of a little girl.

"Hey! Any change?" she called to a passer-by, who turned towards her. She gave them her best smile. After some fumbling in their pocket, a small coin joined the others in the cap she was holding.

Over the course of the afternoon, more smiles at strangers produced more coins. She decanted another handful into one of her pockets. It had taken a few hours, but it had been worthwhile. At a guess she nearly had enough now, and she'd be able to go home.

A big rotund businessman in a suit paused at the kerb, waiting to cross the street. He looked like he might have money. She sidled across to him and tugged gently at his jacket.

"Any change Sir?" she said, putting her head slightly to one side in an attempt to look cute.

She had met another little girl here once and learned a lot, especially about the art of dealing with people.

The man turned slowly to face her. He had untidy white hair and was wearing a bow-tie. He pushed his glasses down his nose with one finger and looked at her over the rim. He reminded her of a wise old owl.

"What for?" he said gently.

She had learned enough about people to know that he was going to give her money, probably folding money she thought. He just wanted an answer to his question. It was a test. It didn't matter what the answer was.

There were many things she could have made up in reply, but the truth seemed good enough. She looked up at him with her big dark eyes and grubby face.

"For the little girl who saved the world?" she asked, quietly.

***

The Council were supposed to provide services, so that Aylas could get on with the business of creating and running worlds, and not have to worry about trivialities. Few of them worked properly, but one service that was not provided by The Council did work flawlessly, and it was an especially useful one.

Life was much easier when you could get on with doing the hard work and leave some of the tidying up to someone else. After all, you couldn't be good at everything. Some things had to be done with flair and elegance, and were best left to a professional.

Jennifer crossed to her message board and touched a little cartouche with the symbol 'K' in the middle of it, which began to glow faintly.

There was unfinished business.

This service was provided by another specific type of creature. In common with almost every other Ayla, she used it regularly. It was a valuable tool. She had never known how it came to exist until she had read the old book properly, but she'd always had a way to call on its services, and now she knew where it came from. Who'd have guessed! It took some of the magic out of the process, but it was much more rewarding when you knew how it worked. Its symbol had only ever been drawn once. After it had been created it could go anywhere and everywhere, in all worlds, never seemed to get fed up, never seemed to appear stressed. That was because it enjoyed its job, which was to make sure that all the deeds across all the worlds in all the universes balanced out.

There was only one of them because one was all you needed, and every good Ayla had it on her message board.

The service it provided was free of charge, very efficient, and didn't take long to arrive.

After scarcely a moment had passed, ripples began to appear in the air near the entrance to the room, and a figure wearing a soft white dress adorned with lace began to emerge from nothingness. If you were searching for words, it could only be described as a vision of beauty. A smiling face with captivating green eyes, surrounded by masses of flaming red hair which curled around its face. Had it been carrying a wand, it could have easily passed for a fairy godmother.

"So, what can I do for you today, Jennifer Marlow?" asked the vision, kindly, after it had finished materialising.

"I need something, and I have something to give," she said, indicating an object on the table beside them.

The vision looked towards it, and treated her to a gentle smile.

"I'm listening," she said.

Jennifer told her, and the vision extended both her hands. Jennifer took them and closed her eyes.

"So, this is what I'd like you to do," she said quietly, making herself a picture in her mind. It was fairly easy to imagine.

"Yes, I understand," said the vision softly after a moment.

"...and this is where you need to go," continued Jennifer without opening her eyes, the lines of concentration rippling across her face as she conjured up the best memory she could of the place, and time, which was a lot more difficult. "Is that good enough? Have you got it?"

"Yes."

She opened her eyes, let go of the vision's hands, and produced a leaflet from her pocket, together with a piece of paper and a pen.

"And a note with it please," she said, holding out the leaflet. The vision took it. "Can you write in this language?"

The vision unfolded the green leaflet, and began to examine the complicated words on it carefully.

"Yes..." it replied with a smile. "I do believe I can. What would you like to say?"

There were many things Jennifer could have made up to say, but the truth seemed good enough.

***

The lady in the tea room put the pen back behind her ear, cleared a table, and took the dishes through to the kitchen at the rear of the shop. She wiped the sweat off her forehead with the back of her wrist, and started to wash up.

Life was hard, but they managed to survive. At least she was able to pay for her son to go to school these days, but the business still had debts. It didn't make a lot of money, but it all helped. On the whole it was a good existence. It was probably best to be grateful for anything at all, she thought, even if it wasn't perfect.

She heard the sound of the entrance door opening, and stuck her head around the end of the wall which separated the kitchen from the seating area, but she couldn't see anyone. People didn't shut it properly. It must have just blown off the latch in the wind, she thought. It was nearly time to close up anyway. She put her tea towel over her shoulder and went to lock up.

On her way past the corner of the counter she noticed something odd about the trays. One of them was empty. There were no Eccles Cakes! Someone had stolen *all* the Eccles Cakes! She ran to the door and flung it open. There were few people in the street at this time of evening anyway, and no obvious Thief of Eccles Cakes.

She shouted an anguished curse, hurled the tea towel down on the ground, and slammed the door with a thump that shook the whole building. Life was hard enough without people stealing from her. Those were meant for tomorrow! She would have to spend her evening baking more now!

After locking the door, she turned, ready to stamp back across the floor and get a clean cloth for wiping the rest of the tables, but stopped dead in her tracks.

In the middle of the counter near the till was a small bag. It hadn't been there when she'd taken some dishes through a few minutes earlier.

She walked over and prodded it gingerly, as if she expected it to explode, before picking it up carefully. It was heavy.

After looking around suspiciously to reassure herself that no-one else was there, she untied the drawstring neck and turned it upside down.

Hundreds of coins spilled across the counter and rattled onto the floor.

She scooped as many of them up into a little heap as she could. It wasn't easy to say how much money there was without counting it properly, but more than a week's takings she would venture. The bag wasn't even empty, there was some folding money in it as well.

And in the bottom of the bag was a note, written carefully in the most beautiful ornate handwriting that she had ever seen.

The message was very simple. It read:

From the little girl who didn't pay

23 - New Council

Jennifer moved her mug, which scratched awkwardly on the gritty table.

"So," she said. "Welcome to the first meeting of the new council".

Jennifer and Alkira were seated in the only two proper chairs, which were adequate, but somewhat hard and uncomfortable after they had been occupied for more than a couple of minutes.

The other three members took the opportunity to shuffle their makeshift stools up closer so they could put their elbows on the table top.

"It's a long time since we were all together in one place," said Ayla Mythros.

"Yes," muttered Ayla Goodison. "About time. We're almost like a little family again."

The others agreed.

"First order of business then," exclaimed Jennifer, pushing a shallow, square tin into the centre of the table.

Four faces craned to view the contents.

Ayla Mubara picked out some kind of flat object, and held is suspiciously in front of her face.

"Some kind of... biscuit?" she ventured.

"They're called Eccles Cakes," replied Jennifer. "They don't look very exciting, but trust me, they are delicious."

"Oh!" exclaimed Ayla Mubara. "I've got crumbs in my tea now!"

Jennifer shot her a stare, and the group burst into laughter.

"You got me there!" exclaimed Jennifer. "I thought for one moment you were serious." Her friend chuckled. "Second order of business then – are we happy with this organisation?"

The other four Aylas exchanged glances.

"Well, I think that we ought to give up the formalities and just call each other by our first names," said Chandra Mythros.

The others nodded, and grunted their approval as they helped themselves to cakes.

"Good choice!" exclaimed Chandra, licking some crumbs off her lip.

"Wonderful then!" said Alkira. "But do you think we'll be accepted by the community? We have no bodyguards if people decide they don't like us."

Jennifer thought about that for a moment.

"There will always be people who'll want to kill us. They'll either hate us because they believe we're doing a bad job, or they'll hate us because they resent the fact that we're doing a good job."

"I suppose so," said Chandra, sadly. "We'll just have to learn to defend ourselves."

"Jennifer knows all about that," said Alkira. "She knows how to defeat almost any attacker."

"Yes," said Jennifer, holding up her hand to Alkira for a high-five.

Alkira thought for a moment.

"Eyeballs?" she asked.

"Yes!" replied Jennifer.

The two Aylas laughed.

"Oh!" sighed Alkira, sadly. "We'll miss her."

"We will," replied Jennifer. "But her memory lives on."

"Can you ever reach those worlds again without their drawings, if you did want to go back?" asked Alkira. "I suppose the bucket of water with all the sludge off the wall would have been no use even if you'd kept it?"

"No, I don't think it would," replied Jennifer, who had reached into her pocket and was bringing out a small stone and a piece of paper with smudges on it. "But these might be."

"What's on the paper?" asked Belinda, craning her neck to see the coloured streaks.

"A rubbing of a little section of wall before I washed everything away," replied Jennifer. "The link between the two sets of worlds isn't completely broken in both directions so long as some part of it remains – however small. With an object from the other world such as this stone with lichen on it, actual life from that world, I think I can probably manage to go there, and with some of the colours from the drawings it might be possible to reverse-engineer it, in some form."

There was a mutter of approval from the others, although Jennifer wasn't convinced they really understood what 'reverse-engineering' was.

"Where did you get the water from to wash the drawing off the wall?" asked Alkira thoughtfully.

"There was already enough in the bucket," replied Jennifer. "I didn't need to go looking for any more. Why?"

"I see," said Alkira, thoughtfully. "And, did it happen to be... yellow... by any chance?"

Jennifer squinted at her through half-closed eyes, and then looked slowly and meaningfully at each expressionless face around the table in turn.

A short, silent pause followed for the refilling of mugs, and the acquisition of more Eccles Cakes.

"These are nice!" exclaimed Belinda. "Can you get more of them for the next meeting?"

"Oh yes!" exclaimed Jennifer, brightly. "I know how to get money that works in that world now, and I'm sure my supplier will be glad of ongoing future business."

"It doesn't seem right," said Mabel. "Just the five of us, I mean."

"I agree. Six is the magic number," said Alkira. "It's the only one that makes any sense."

"Yes, I think so too," agreed Jennifer. "But where do we get another sensible, reliable person who will do justice to the responsibility of putting the best interests of all the worlds first, and who will work hard and not necessarily expect too much in return?"

As she was saying this, she was turning her head slowly towards the open kitchen door. The others watched her with interest, and nodded silently.

"JEFFERSON!" she shouted.

After a moment, the old man's head appeared round the door frame.

"Yes Miss? Do you need more tea?"

"No, but thank you," replied Jennifer, kindly. "We're about to start running the universe properly. I think we can manage to make our own tea."

"Oh yes Miss. Of course. Er... what do you want then?"

Jennifer momentarily glanced around at the others for any sign that they were going to be unhappy with what she was about to say, before turning back to look into his eyes.

"Would you like..." she said softly, "...a job?"

24 - Picnic Spot

Mister Pluto sat motionless on the window sill, looking out across the city. There was a lot more activity here compared to his old home in the garret. The streets were full of people, the air smelled of strange foods, and he was sure he could smell mice, and probably rats. Jennifer had called round again today, and he was keeping out of the way. The thought of being close to something that looked like a human being, but who could turn itself into an apparition that didn't exist and go around looking at paintings when it had no eyes, made his fur stand on end. He was determined to avoid direct eye contact in case her abilities extended to the creation of sculpture. He was also hungry, but his servant was talking to her about some things called a 'holiday planner' and a 'critical path'. He didn't know what those things were, but they didn't sound edible.

Getting a new council to work properly had been easier than Jennifer had expected. The others were definitely up for making big changes. The physical ones would be easy, but the biggest challenge would be to improve the way The Council were perceived. They would need to find a new meeting place, there simply wasn't the space or the facilities for them to meet here at Jefferson's apartment, and they probably needed a new name as well. The list had steadily grown longer over the week, and although there was a lot to do there were still a couple of loose ends to tie up.

"Thank you for the help with the painting," said Jennifer, looking across at the frame which was still perched on its easel near the wall. "We must put it somewhere safe."

"Good of you to say so, but I don't really like it," replied the old man. "It looks somehow unreal. I can't put my finger on it. It's good for a first effort but I don't think anybody would buy it."

Jennifer regarded it with a critical gaze. To an eye trained in the subtle art of bringing drawings to life, the red and white sign on the inn seemed to pop out from the surroundings, and the dim yellow glow visible through the windows of the hall flickered almost imperceptibly. It still looked good to her.

"Just wrap it up and put it in the cupboard then, if you don't like it," she said, unemotionally. "It doesn't matter. We don't need to keep it on display. It just needs to be stored somewhere safe, for about twenty or thirty years." The old man nodded. "Help me drag this around here a bit," she continued, turning her attention to one of the concrete chairs. "We need to get rid of all this to make room for something more comfortable for you."

Jefferson took hold of one of the solid arms, and together they pulled it forwards nearer the table, and spun it round a bit, making a grating and screeching noise as it raked across the wooden floor. Mister Pluto yowled, and fled into the bathroom in search of a peaceful place to sleep.

She stood back and considered the layout.

"And the other chair needs to go that way a smidgen, and turned round to face the table too."

The heavy furniture was hard to handle, but she knew it would be much easier to move here where the surface was smooth, rather than waiting until they got where they were going.

"You can come with me if you like," she said brightly after they had finished, and she was happy with the layout.

Jefferson thought he would. It was always nice to go to different places, and see new things, especially if it meant holding Jennifer's hand. Travelling wasn't something he'd ever had the chance to do. There was a whole world out there to see, in fact there were countless worlds to see. More worlds than you could ever imagine. After all, you were never too old to start new adventures.

They closed their eyes and Jennifer imagined the space around her, and where and when she wanted to be. It was hard, dragging lumps of concrete across the boundaries of worlds through time and space. The few boulders that she had inadvertently picked up at the site of the car crash had seemed lightweight by comparison.

Jefferson didn't weigh much because he was willing and conscious and didn't have to be dragged.

She opened her eyes. Yes, that had worked! She wasn't losing her touch. There were the skid marks and the scratches of paint on the rock. She nudged him with her elbow, and he opened his eyes, blinking in the sunlight.

"We're here."

"Oh! It's very nice, just as you described it," he said after a moment.

Letting go of her hand, he walked to the edge of the ridge and looked down into the valley, across the plain to the forests and the river that snaked off around the curve of the big hill on its way to the sea.

"So that's where the little girl lives now is it? Very nice." He studied the details carefully. "It would make a good landscape."

"Yes, I think it would," replied Jennifer. "Remember the details carefully, and we'll see if you can learn to find your way back here one day on your own. We can work on that, but in the meantime, I'm happy to bring you here whenever you want to paint it."

He looked worried.

"And take me back again?" he asked.

"And take you back again," she said with a smile.

"What are you going to do with all this concrete furniture?"

Jennifer looked up at the shafts of light sparkling through the canopy of green leaves that fluttered against the background of deep blue sky.

"We'll leave it right here," she said. "It's a lovely place for a picnic spot and," she added thoughtfully, "a fitting memorial to someone's daddy who I couldn't save."

Jefferson looked up at the sky too. It really was a beautiful world.

"Good idea Miss Jennifer," he said. "Isn't life strange. I never really wanted much to do with you, but you're a lovely girl now I've got to know you better. I saw you for all those years at the council meetings, and for some reason I always thought your name was Jacqueline."

Jennifer gave him a smile, and held out her hand.

"Shall we go on an adventure?" she said.